DEATH CANYON

DEATH CANYON

•

Howard Pelham

AVALON BOOKS
NEW YORK

PRINTED IN THE UNITED STATES OF AMERICA
ON ACID-FREE PAPER
BY HADDON CRAFTSMEN, BLOOMSBURG, PENNSYLVANIA

To Jim Meals:
a good agent, a good friend.

Chapter One

Scott Golden rode into Dodge City, Kansas at mid-afternoon. Pulling up before the Driscoll Livery, he swung down and turned his horse, Big Red, over to a man with auburn hair, light skin, and a nice harvest of freckles across his cheeks and nose.

"The name is Tom Driscoll," the man said, offering Scott his hand.

"Scott Golden." He shook Driscoll's hand. "I'd like to leave my horse here."

"You've brought 'em to the right place. Looks like he's been traveling hard. I'll give 'em a good currying and a bag of oats."

"He'd appreciate both, I'm sure," Scott said, dragging his rifle from its boot and reaching for his saddle-bags.

"How long will you be staying?" Driscoll asked.

"Just overnight."

1

"I'll lock your tack in the office there, and your friend here will be ready and waiting at sunup."

"I want a bed for the night myself. Can you recommend a place to stay?" Scott asked.

"That hotel just down the street there." Driscoll pointed at a two-story unpainted building half a block away. "The Belvedere. Sounds a lot fancier than it is, but the place is clean and cheap."

"Sounds like what I need. Thanks."

Carrying his rifle and saddlebags, Scott walked the half block and upon entering the hotel registered at a desk officiated by an aging clerk with slumping shoulders, gray thinning hair, and weak blue eyes.

"Number 201," the man said. "That's upstairs overlooking the street."

The room was small but neat and clean. Scott put his saddlebags and rifle on a table that already held a coal oil lamp, opened the window, and glanced down at the street. A few pedestrians hurried along, and a wagon loaded with feed rumbled by. Turning away, he crossed to the bed and stretched out without removing his six-gun. His intent was to rest only for a little while, but he soon dropped off to sleep.

Scott Golden was a little over six feet, 190 pounds. His features were a little too sharp to be called handsome. But his face showed strength, something everyone who met him respected. Men seemed uneasy with the strength that emanated from him. What they sensed, though none understood it, was a mettle in the man that would brook no opposition when he knew he was right.

*   *   *

Scott woke up in the dark, struck a match, and, crossing to the table on which he'd left his rifle and saddlebags, lit the lamp. The sounds of Dodge City nightlife drifted in through the window, reminding Scott of how hungry and thirsty he was. A washstand with pitcher and bowl sat against one wall. He took a drink directly from the pitcher and emptied the rest of the water into the bowl. He washed his face, dried off, and then beat as much dust as he could from his shirt and pants. Then he left the room, locked the door, and went downstairs.

He stood outside the hotel a moment, listening to the tinny sound of a piano coming from a nearby saloon. The strong smell of roasting beef drew him along the street. When he came to the cafe, he went in and sat at the counter.

"Bring me a steak and all the trimmings," he told the middle-aged woman who took his order.

When his food arrived, he dug in, and he decided he had never eaten a meal that tasted so good. Sopping the last of the gravy with a hot biscuit and emptying his coffee cup for the third time, he stood up, paid the lady, and exited into the street. Music still came from the saloon, and now the piano was accompanied by a woman singing *Only A Bird In A Gilded Cage*. Deciding he'd stop in at the saloon and listen to the singing, he headed up the street. He was passing a dark alley when a man stepped out of the shadows and poked a gun into his ribs.

"You're coming with me," the man said, and guided Scott into the alley.

Thinking of the money belt around his waist and the few dollars in his pocket, Scott thought of trying to resist.

"Don't try nothing!" the thief snapped, as though reading Scott's mind. "You make me shoot you, and I'll shoot to kill."

A chill from a threat that had the ring of truth about it hummed along Scott's spine. "What do you want?" he asked.

"I want your money."

"I'll get it if you'll let me put my hand in my pocket."

"Go ahead, but you bring anything else out, you're a dead man."

Slipping a hand into his pocket, Scott brought out several pieces of gold. "That's all," he said, hoping the man would believe him.

The man, still only a hulking shadow, took the money and stuffed it into his own pocket. Then he jammed the gun barrel into Scott's side a little harder and began to pat Scott down. "I'll take that, too," he said upon finding the money belt. Scott had no choice but to open his shirt, unbuckle the money belt, and hand it over. The man took the belt and ordered Scott to face the street. Then Scott felt a blow to his head. Shooting stars exploded in his brain.

When he finally pushed himself up, he was alone in the alley. Clinging to the wall for support, he stumbled out of the alley and walked unsteadily down the street to his hotel. The clerk was nowhere to be seen as he made his way up the stairs and to his room. He was thankful he still had the room key. Opening the door, he staggered to the bed, lowered himself to the mattress, and passed out.

Scott Golden had a terrible headache when he awoke. He lay for a moment wondering about the pain, and then everything came back to him. After a minute, he pushed himself up. When the room ceased to spin, he made it to the mirror over the washstand. His hair was coated with dried blood and his fingers explored a knot the size of an egg on the back of his head. However, that seemed the extent of his injury. Shards of sunlight cut into the room. He had slept all night. By the time Golden managed to make himself presentable, his stomach was growling for breakfast.

Then he realized he had no money for food.

Realizing the hopelessness of his situation, he almost gave way to panic. Then his mind began to work. He could sell something. But what? His gaze lighted on the rifle on the table beside his saddlebags. He headed for the streets again, found a gun shop and went in. The owner stood in the back of the shop before a machine that held a six-gun tightly in its grip, filing away at the six-gun's trigger. Noticing Scott, he stopped what he was doing and came to the front.

"Could I help you, sir?"

"I'm looking to sell my rifle," Scott said.

"A man has to be mighty needful to sell his gun," the gunsmith observed. "You in some kind of trouble, fella? Maybe I can help?"

The man had such a kindly look in his eyes, Scott knew he was serious. "Got a gun stuck in my gut and was forced into an alley last night. Guy took all my money. I'd appreciate it if you could give me as much as you can on the rifle."

"How much are you asking?"

"It belonged to my pa. Say fifty dollars."

The gunsmith reached for the rifle, held the stock to his shoulder, and sighted along the barrel. "Can't go that high," he said, "but I will go twenty-five. Hope that'll do you some good."

Scott thought of refusing, but the energy he had expended getting from his room to the gun shop made him faint with hunger.

"All right," he said.

Stuffing the money into his pocket, he turned back to the street and, finding a cafe, ordered coffee, pancakes, and ham. He lingered over the coffee and considered where he would go from here and how far $24.20 would take him. Not very far, he decided. He needed to make more money somehow. But how?

Maybe a poker game? That's what an old friend of his would have advised. A friend who also taught him some things about drawing a gun.

Feeling one hundred percent better on a full stomach, he rose, paid his bill, and left the cafe. The stores had just begun to open as he wandered along the streets looking for a likely saloon. He went into the first saloon he found. A barkeep, his clothes so fresh Scott knew he had just come on duty, was busy wiping the bar. At a table in the rear three men sat around a poker table covered in green felt. A stubble of beard covered their faces, and half-smoked cigars smoldered on ashtrays, the smoke drifting lazily to the ceiling.

Obviously, the game was a holdover from the night before.

Scott walked back to the table, but stayed far enough away so as not to disturb the players. "May I sit in?" he asked after watching a couple of hands.

All eyes turned on him. "Why, he's just a kid," one man said.

"You got money?" asked another.

"Yes, sir."

"Then I don't see why not."

The game was five card stud, and the ante a dollar. Scott drew a king down, and raised the bet a dollar when his turn came. The others called his bet, but the succeeding cards were a washout for Scott, and he lost five dollars before he dropped out.

His next down card was a deuce, his first up card another. Scott's pulse quickened as he drew a nine, another deuce and, finally, another nine. Only after he received the last nine did he begin to raise the bet, but not high enough to cause the others to drop out. Scott's up cards showed two pairs: deuces and nines. On the final bet, he called and raised ten dollars.

"Too rich for me," one man said, tossing in his cards.

"Me, too," said another.

The third man, a large, dark-complexioned man with deep-set eyes, showed pairs of kings and fours. He studied his cards a moment and said, "You're trying to bluff me, kid," and tossed a twenty-dollar gold piece on the table.

Scott called.

"That's it," the man said. "What you got down?"

He gave a grunt of disappointment when Scott turned over another deuce. "That cleaned me out," he said, and pushed back from the table.

"I gotta go, too," said another.

"Me, too," said the third.

Scott sat at the table and counted up his winnings, which came to one hundred and fifty-three dollars.

The barkeep approached to clean the table. "Looks like you did all right, sir," he said.

"Just luck, I guess," Scott replied.

Scott returned to the gun shop and waited for the gunsmith to come to the front again.

"You again?" the man said, recognizing Scott.

"I've come for my rifle." Scott placed twenty-five dollars on the counter.

"Not so fast, son," the gunsmith said and smiled. "How did you come by that money? You didn't knock someone on the head for it, did you?"

"Got into a poker game," Scott said.

"Where?"

"In the saloon down the street."

"You won money off that gang down there?" the gunsmith asked. "That bunch is almost professional. Where did you learn to play poker so well?"

"You ever heard of Doc Holiday?"

"Who hasn't heard of Doc? He stayed around Dodge for years before he traipsed off to New Mexico."

"Doc taught me the game."

The gunsmith laughed. "I bet you didn't tell those fellas in the saloon before they let you into the game."

"No."

The gunsmith looked at the money in Scott's hand. "Since you're so flush, you can have your rifle back for thirty dollars."

Scott smirked and added five dollars to the money on the counter.

The gunsmith picked up the money, reached for Scott's rifle, and passed it over the counter to him.

Back on the street, Golden returned to the hotel and picked up the rest of his things. Tom Driscoll had just finished saddling Scott's horse when he arrived, once again carrying a rifle and his saddle bags.

"Thought you'd be along right soon," Driscoll said, giving the horse a gentle slap on his withers.

"Well, so long," Scott paid the man and climbed into Big Red's saddle.

"Where you headed now?" the hostler asked.

"No place in particular."

Once beyond Dodge, Scott turned west. He'd lived in the Rocky Mountains once and decided he'd like to see them again.

Chapter Two

Night was approaching, and lemon, gold, and red light brushed the bottoms of the puffy clouds floating over the peaks of the Rocky Mountains where the sun was about to set. Scott Golden was more than two weeks out of Dodge City. Traveling south along the foothills, he began to look for a place to camp. The mouth of a canyon running back into the foothills caught his attention.

"Whoa, Red," he said to the horse.

The canyon stretched at least a half mile back into the foothills. A line of cottonwood and willows began at the rear and ran almost to the mouth of the canyon and then came to an abrupt halt.

"Got to be water in those trees," Scott Golden murmured to the horse and spurred the animal into the canyon.

Indeed, there was water. Drainage off the tall snow-covered peaks formed a small stream that emptied into the canyon and spread out left and right, providing water for the thick grass and the trees. Well before reaching the mouth of the canyon, the little stream disappeared into the loamy soil of the canyon.

Scott Golden chose a spot beneath a cottonwood beside the tiny flow of water. Stripping Big Red of his tack, he led the horse to a rich patch of grass and staked him out to graze. Then he returned to the campsite and took a coffee pot from the provision sack and set it aside. Next, he gathered a handful of dried grass and twigs, struck a match, and stuck it to the grass. As the flame built, he gathered a few dead limbs and placed them crosswise over the fire. Filling the coffeepot from the tiny stream, he set it beside the fire. Returning to the provision sack, he rummaged through its contents, extracting a can of sardines and a small container of crackers. For twenty minutes he ate sardines and crackers and washed the food down with black coffee.

The month was August, argued by some to be Colorado's hottest. But the night still seemed cool to Scott, and he had never slept more comfortably, soothed in part by the soft flap of cottonwood leaves stirred by a slight breeze and the trickling of the nearby stream.

He awoke the following morning feeling rested and refreshed. Saddling Big Red, he circled the canyon, liking what he saw. When he found no other exit but the one through which he had entered the night before, he liked the canyon even better. A box canyon with only one entrance, rich with grass, shade, and water was ideal for raising cattle. A ranch set in the canyon could easily be handled by one man alone. For years Scott Golden had been looking for just such a place, and to stumble over it in such a manner was almost too good to be true.

He stopped in the mouth of the canyon as he rode out and looked back. The early morning sun turned the dew-covered grass into millions of diamonds. Even from where he sat on Big Red he could see the numerous birds among the trees . . . thrush, mockingbirds, magpies, even tiny wrens. Their songs seemed to set the canyon apart for Scott Golden, lending it a touch of something very special. He tried to think what that was, but couldn't put a name to it.

At that moment, he decided to make the canyon his home if someone else had not already laid claim to it. He'd ride into Denver and ask at the land office. If the canyon was still free for homesteading, he'd file a claim. Making careful note of the canyon's location relative to the tallest peak, Scott turned Big Red's head east toward Denver, letting the big horse pick his own way across the rocky ground through patches of mesquite and an occasional cactus.

A brown fog from the many necessary fires required in even a small town like Denver hung over the shallow valley that lay at the edge of an endless plateau stretching south. Scott studied the brown ceiling and sent Big Red down the brief western slope into the town.

He rode along Cherry Creek and was sad to find it was no longer the clear bright stream he remembered from before the miners came. Though the gold had long since been sifted from the banks and the stream bed, the damage remained. Not only had the banks been decimated, but the trees were gone as well, giving the once beautiful stream a ravaged look.

Across the trickle that was Cherry Creek, Denver City had a lusty air of brawling, uncouth growth. On all sides were the naked skeletons of buildings in various stages of finish. The high whine of a sawmill filled the air, and amid the babble of voices and the sucking of hoofs lifting from the mud came the constant banging of hammers pounding nails, of handsaws, of iron sledge against iron stake. At McGee Street a new bridge now spanned the creek, at least some sign of progress, Scott decided. At Blake stood another, far too flimsy-looking and tilted in the middle.

From Wazee to the Platte, half-hidden by cottonwoods, stretched hundreds of tents, wagons, and lean-to shacks. An Indian village was dominated by children playing at a game Golden couldn't identify. Between the Indian village and town were three wagon trains drawn into rough circles.

Crude hand-painted signs hung outside many of the buildings. Scott rode to a familiar one that read LAND OFFICE, and pulled Big Red up before a short pole that served as a hitch rack.

Lifting a leg and sliding from Big Red's saddle, he scraped his boots on the boardwalk before the office, pushed the door in, and entered. A long counter blocked his way. Stopping, he looked past the counter to a man who sat behind a desk studying some papers.

"Hello, Harry," Scott Golden said.

The man turned. "Why, Scott!" he exclaimed and,

pushing back from the desk, came to the counter and reached for Scott's hand. "Haven't seen you since last Christmas. How have you been and what have you been doing?"

Harry Poston was a thin man, and his height, close to six feet, made him appear thinner than he was. He was losing his hair in front, and combed it over the balding spot from the left side. His three-piece suit had a rumpled look.

"I'm fine," replied Scott. "How're Glory and the kids?"

"Couldn't be better. You got business? Or you just visiting? Glory's about got some food ready. You'll have to stay and eat."

"I never was able to turn one of Glory's meals down. You know that, Harry."

"But I take it you didn't just come to eat."

"No. I came across a canyon in the foothills I liked the sight of. I was wondering if anybody had laid claim to it."

"Well, let's see." Harry Poston turned and walked to a table in the rear of the office and searched among the many papers. He returned to the counter and spread a map before Scott. "Show me," he said.

Scott studied the mountain range for a moment and placed his forefinger on the spot. "Right there," he said.

Harry Poston studied the map and returned to his desk and opened a book. He found a page and studied it for a moment. "I'm afraid it's been claimed, Scott," he said.

"Who?" Scott asked.

"Jonathan Sampson. You know him?"

"I've seen him around from time to time. He's the man with all those sons, isn't he?"

"Four sons," replied Poston. "All as mean as the old man, or so I've been told."

"I guess Jonathan Sampson filed on the canyon during the gold rush," Scott said. "Probably figured gold would be found along the foothills."

Poston worked his hands nervously, then spoke in a soft voice. "Folks talk about a gent who planned to file on that property before the Sampsons took heed of it. Seems this fellow was a nice enough man but he talked too much. His body was found out there before he could file. The official story is that his horse threw him. Nobody can prove otherwise."

"But I'll bet Jonathan Sampson filed on that property shortly after the body was found."

"You bet right. Ever since that place has been known as Death Canyon." Poston's words produced a grim silence that didn't last long.

"Food is ready, Harry," Glory Poston said, coming into the office through a back door that Scott knew led to their living quarters. Seeing Scott, she exclaimed, "Why, you're here just right to eat with us, Scott! You did invite him, didn't you Harry?"

"Of course."

"Then come on and wash up."

They bathed their hands in a basin just outside the back door, drying them off on a clean flour sack that served as towel. An array of freshly washed clothes hung on a line across the backyard, flapping gently in a northwestern breeze. A rooster and a few hens pecked and scratched at the ground, and a small mongrel dog the Poston boys called Tiger came from beneath the back steps and sniffed at Scott's foot.

"Get away, Tiger!" Harry Poston scolded.

"Where are the kids?" Scott asked, glancing about the kitchen when they were back inside and seated.

"My sister took them off my hands. She always does that on wash day."

The table held a platter of ham, black eyed peas, and turnip greens. Glory Poston served up hot biscuits and cornbread, and they washed the meal down with some of the best coffee Scott had ever drunk.

"The kids will be disappointed in not seeing you, Scott," Glory said. "You know how much they dote on you."

She was a short, stout woman with graying hair tucked into a ball at the nape of her neck and held in place by a couple of reddish combs. She had brown eyes, at the corners of which were small worry lines. Deeper wrinkles extended across her brow. She looked a little like a bantam hen as she scurried about the kitchen.

"I miss seeing the children too," Scott said. "You tell 'em so when they get home."

"When are you gonna settle down and have kids of your own?" asked Glory. "You're a family man, whether you know it or not."

"Well, I best get back out to the office," Harry said, interrupting his wife's banter and pushing back from the table. "Scott, you stay and talk to Glory as long as you will. She gripes all the time about not having somebody to talk to."

"I do not! I don't complain about anyone not talking but you!" She turned to Scott. "The older he gets the more trouble I have getting anything out of him. You'd think age was crippling his tongue."

Scott laughed. "I remember the time you thought he talked too much, Glory."

"There! You see! You just can't please a woman. You better realize when you're well off, Scott. They talk as sweet as pie before you marry 'em. But once you marry up with them, nothing you do will please them. Oh, for the life of a bachelor once again!"

"You get on out of here," Glory said, slapping her husband on his shoulder, but Scott saw the love she had for him in the gentle blow.

He helped Glory clear the table and dried the dishes as she washed them. She talked continuously as they worked. When they were finished, he kissed her on the forehead. "I better be going, Glory, it was real good. Thanks."

"You could spend the night," Glory offered. "I could put two of the boys on a pallet, and you could use their bed."

Scott had done that often in the past, but something prompted him to refuse the invitation this time.

Feeling great disappointment that the canyon had already been homesteaded, Scott left the kitchen, crossed through the living room, and entered the office.

"Scott, I may have good news. I checked the paperwork again, and the date for building on that property has run out. Did you notice a building of any kind?"

"No, there was no building there."

"Then you can file on it. Let me draw up the papers."

Scott's spirits lifted as quickly as they had sunk. He waited and signed the paper. "You never saw a place like this, Harry," he said to Poston as he wrote. "When I get a cabin up, I'll have you, Glory, and the kids out for a long weekend visit."

"And we'll surely come," Poston said. "And remember, you've got to build on that site by the time those papers say. Otherwise, the homestead claim ain't no good.

"Don't worry, Harry. I gotta have me a cabin to live in."

With the filing finished, Scott said goodbye to Harry Poston and returned to the street. He had intended to ride back to the canyon at once, but decided instead to get a drink. Glory's father was a man whose life had been destroyed by alcohol, and she would tolerate no hard liquor in her home. Scott respected Glory's feelings and to some degree agreed with them. He had witnessed on many occasions what the bottle could do to a man. But he felt excited on this night and wanted something to soothe his nerves. He stepped through the batwing doors of the first saloon he came to, not even bothering to look at the sign out front. He leaned inconspicuously at one end of the bar and quietly ordered a beer. As he drank, he stared out of a small window in the saloon, not really seeing anything.

Only once before in his life had Scott owned a place of any kind, and the memory of that place reminded him of the death of his father, Turner Golden.

He recalled the last day of his father's life. Turner Golden had ridden out to drift their little herd of short-horns nearer to the house. The small ranch lay to the east of Presidio, near the Mexican border, and Mexican bandits made a practice of riding over the border to rustle cattle and kill their owners. For that reason, Turner Golden liked to keep the small herd near the house where he could watch them. For the same reason, he never left the house without his rifle and Colt .44 strapped about his waist.

The sky was cloudless, and the sun had beat down mercilessly on Scott's back that day. Sweat trickled from his forehead into his eyes and down his cheeks. He could feel a drop roll down his spine from time to time. He wiped the sweat from his brow and continued working among the plants in the garden, a chore his father had assigned him before he rode out.

Scott would have much preferred to be with his father, but he continued to work at the hot chore of grubbing the garden.

Then he heard the shots.

Springing to his feet, he looked in the direction from which his father should be coming. A half mile away, riders were bunching the cattle and heading them south. *Bandits!* he thought, and began to run as he saw his father's pinto horse galloping toward the house, the saddle empty. Grabbing the reins, he climbed aboard and rode toward where he knew his father must be. Meanwhile, the small herd of shorthorns were being pushed hard toward the border.

He found his father beyond a slight rise among knee-deep grass and, jumping from the saddle, knelt beside him. "Pa!" he said, giving his father's shoulder a gentle shake. "Pa!" he said again as Turner's eyes opened and he gazed up at his son.

"I'll ride into town for help, Pa! You just lie still."

Turner Golden reached a hand up to Scott's arms and held him. "It's too late, son. Just stay here with me."

"Who was it, Pa? Did you recognize him?"

"You tell the sheriff it was old Jose Conejo himself who shot me." Turner coughed. A slight trickle of blood colored the corners of his mouth. "And Scott?"

"Yes, Pa."

"Do something for me?"

"If I can, Pa."

"Sell this place and get away from here. Your ma died here, and now me. Don't let it be the death of you, too."

"You ain't dying, Pa! And I'm going after Conejo!"

"No, son. That's the last thing I want you to do. You'll get killed, too. Just sell this place and get away from here. Go anywhere—north, east, west. Just leave this place."

Turner Golden took his son's hand. "I hate leaving you like this, son," he said, "but there's nothing I can do about it. You take care of yourself and grow up to be a good man."

Scott watched the life go out of his father's eyes, and sat there a long time holding his father's hand.

He gave his father the kind of funeral he knew he would like, but he hadn't followed his advice. Scott knew he could never live with himself if he rode away without making a final call on Conejo.

Saddened by the memory of his father's murder, Scott finished his drink and hastily left the saloon. He walked to where Big Red was tied, climbed into the saddle, and headed west. He wanted very much to get back to the canyon and begin building his second home.

On his return, he stopped off at Blake Lester's place. Lester came from the barn and watched as Scott rode into the yard and pulled up.

"Step down, Golden. I got some coffee on if you'd like a cup."

"Thanks, but I'll take a rain check. I was wondering if you had any brood cows or heifers you'd like to sell."

"You buying?"

"I am."

"Didn't know you had a place."

"I just filed a homestead claim on a place in the foothills over there." Scott described the canyon.

"Know it. Thought of that place myself, but old Jonathan Sampson had already laid claim to it. You know about that, I reckon."

"His claim expired," Scott replied.

"Does old Sampson and his boys know that?"

"I don't know, but it don't make any difference."

"Sampson might not agree," Lester said, watching Scott's face.

"We'll see," was Scott's reply.

"I could let you have fifteen or so brood cows," Lester said. "You'll be needing a bull as well."

"Thanks, Blake. I'll drive them to the canyon now, if that's all right with you."

"Fine. I'll get my riders to cut them out."

When the cowboys returned, they were herding fifteen brood cows, some with calves at side, a few of these almost at weaning age.

"But Blake . . ." Scott protested. "Calves, too?"

"I want you to be beholdin' to me," Blake Lester laughed as he spoke. "I'll be needin' some more help 'round here, expect a neighborly visit when that happens."

Scott raised one finger to his hat and saluted. "I can tell you're going to make a fine neighbor, Blake. Maybe we can make a habit of trading favors."

As Scott herded the cattle toward the valley, he felt more content than he had in a long time. And he thought of Glory Poston's words. Maybe he did need a wife beside him.

He drove the little herd into the canyon and watched them spread out. Soon they were grazing leisurely on grass that reached to their bellies. He wondered if he should set up camp at the canyon entrance. But after studying a few of the older cows for awhile, he was sure they would remain where they were.

Some had already found the stream and now lay under the cottonwoods, chewing their cuds. They were acting as if they'd found a new home and liked what they'd found.

Chapter Three

"**Y**ou've done a fine job with this ranch." Anne Barber lifted an eyebrow slyly as she looked down at Golden from her black mare. "It's a fine place for horses and cows. Perhaps you should give some thought to making it suitable for two-legged animals."

Anne smiled at her own joke. Scott liked the way she smiled, even when he sensed that the joke was on him. He struggled to think of something funny to say back to her. He was still struggling when she spoke again.

"Aren't you going to invite me in? I brought you a special gift for your new cabin."

"Oh sure," he replied. "But the cabin isn't all that new. Had it for, oh, nine months or so, now. Course, I've added on to it some since you and your father visited last fall."

Anne was off her horse and pulling something from the saddle bags. She handed a book, *Three Tragedies*

By Shakespeare, to Scott. "I was very impressed by your library on my first visit. I hope this will make a nice addition."

"Thanks, thanks a lot. I do love books. Probably the smartest thing I ever did was buying books from that drummer that came through town, nothin' else to do here at night 'cept read."

Anne looked at the ground. Sensing he had committed a social gaffe, or something close to it, Scott hastily continued. "Ah, won't you please come in?"

Scott felt jubilant when he saw the look of approval on Anne's face as she stepped into the cabin. "This is remarkable, Mr. Golden," she said. "To think you did this all in one winter, along with the barn and corrals."

"Blake Lester lent a hand. We help each other out some."

They were standing in the front room of the cabin, a room dominated by a large stone fireplace in which latent embers still smoldered. A rocker and two straight chairs sat before the fireplace. Made by Golden from soft pine, their seats were fashioned from strips of cowhide, hair side up. A narrow table took up most of one wall and held an open Bible. Behind the Bible was a small row of books. Among the titles were *Pilgrim's Progress*, Homer's *Iliad* and *Odyssey*, and the novels of Sir Walter Scott. All of James Fenimore Cooper's *Leatherstocking Tales* were included, along with Hawthorne's *The Scarlet Letter*, and several of Charles Dickens' novels.

Two doors led to a kitchen and bedroom.

Golden placed the Shakespeare at the end of the row of books beside *Oliver Twist*. "I haven't read Shakespeare yet, but about two years ago I saw the play *Hamlet* in Denver. It didn't go too well. There were some pretty rough fellows there who kept shouting at the actors, especially the women actors. I guess it made them nervous. I read in the paper the next day that they cut out a large part of the play."

"I imagine touring through the west can be hard on actors," Anne said.

"Did you go to the theater much when you were at school in Boston, Miss Barber?"

"Oh yes." Anne's face glowed. "I love the theater."

"Do you miss the east?"

Anne's voice was firm. "Yes, I miss some things, of course. But I am where I belong. What about you, Mr. Golden, do you feel you belong here on this ranch?"

For some reason the question startled Golden and made him feel even more nervous. He stammered out a "Yes."

"That doesn't surprise me. You've done so much with this place in just eight months. I hope you don't think the Barbers are unfriendly. I wanted to come by again sooner, at least to wish you a Merry Christmas, but winter came early and was so brutal." She paused briefly, then continued, "And Father, well, fathers can be finicky sometimes, you know."

Scott knew all right. Dan Barber was a very wealthy and powerful rancher. He was friendly enough in his own way. After all, he had come by the previous September with his daughter to say hello and to wish Scott good luck. But he wouldn't want his daughter wasting her time on a struggling saddle tramp.

As he thought about it, Scott guessed that he couldn't blame the man.

The mention of her father seemed to put Anne in a slightly somber mood. "I guess I have bothered you long enough, Mr. Golden."

"You haven't bothered me at all, Miss Barber."

An awkward silence followed. Scott desperately wanted to think of something to keep Anne at the ranch for a little while longer. All he could come up with was inviting her to have a look at the barn. But he was reluctant to try that. The barn was just a barn. Nothing special. He was sure the barn on the Barber ranch was much better.

Anne shrugged her shoulders. "Well, as Shakespeare would say, 'Exit, stage left.' "

They both laughed self-consciously as Anne left the cabin and mounted her horse. After she had left, Scott busied himself around the barn and corrals doing minor chores, trying to quell the restless feeling Anne's visit had given him. About an hour had passed when he decided to return to the cabin and make himself a pot of coffee. Of course! He should have offered Anne some coffee. He entered the cabin muttering to himself and wondering if Anne thought he was being deliberately rude because he didn't offer her anything.

Before he could get started on the coffee, Scott heard the approach of riders. He walked to the front of the cabin where he could see the entrance to the canyon. He watched five riders enter, ride to where he stood, and pull up.

"Good day, Mr. Sampson," he said. "Will you and your boys step down? I was just getting started on a pot of coffee." Scott watched as the Sampson boys spread out on either side of their father.

"We ain't come for a friendly visit," Jonathan Sampson said. "We come to tell you to git outta this canyon. It's ours. We ain't searched it solidly for gold yet. Now that it's spring the time has come."

Jonathan Sampson was a heavyset, broad-faced man with angry eyes, black graying hair, and a black beard streaked with gray. He and his sons had obviously come with the intent of running Scott out of the canyon.

"Harry Poston told me your claim had expired," Scott said, his gaze covering all five of the Sampsons.

"Told me the same thing," the old man replied. "But that don't make no difference. This place is ours. Now you pack up and git, 'fore we have to do something you won't like at all."

The four Sampson sons laughed, as though their father had just said something quite witty.

Boyd, the eldest, was a carbon copy of his father: broad face, black hair, and black beard. Physically, Yancey Sampson, the second son, had inherited his mother's features. Blond, slender, sometimes mistaken for a dude because of his flashy dress, he was known to be more vicious than even his brother Boyd. No man in the West was more dangerous with a knife. Champ Sampson, the third son, had earned the nickname from his love of fistfighting. A dark, heavyset brute of a man, he had been in the ring for a brief time. Blackie, the youngest, just missed being handsome. He had the same dark features as his father, but somehow they had come together in a different fashion in the youngest son. Blackie had quite a way with women, or so Scott had heard.

Without warning, Scott dropped his hand to the butt of his .44, and for a moment there was absolute quiet. Somewhere overhead a crow cawed, and the wind rattled the leaves of the nearby cottonwood. Even the tinkling of the stream could be heard in the tense silence.

"Clear out, Mr. Sampson, and take your boys with you," Scott said, his voice even but deadly serious. "I own this valley now, and it's all legal. If you ever set foot in here again, you better come as a friend."

"Let's take him, Pa," Boyd Sampson urged. "He may draw that gun, but we'll kill 'em before he can shoot any of us."

"I'd think twice if I were you before giving that order, Mr. Sampson. You'll surely kill me, but I'll get at least one shot off, and guess who I'll be shooting at. You don't want to make orphans of these poor boys of yours, do you? They appear to need the steadying hand of an older man."

After that the silence continued for a moment longer. Then Jonathan Sampson placed his hands on the horn of his saddle. "Another time, boys," he said, and swung his mount around.

The four Sampson sons followed suit.

"We'll be back!" Boyd Sampson yelled, turning his head to look at Scott. "You can depend on that, Golden!"

Scott watched them go. I may have to kill them before they kill me, he thought to himself. Though there had been times when he had been forced to kill or be killed, killing anything, especially another human being, was something abhorrent to him. I wish I could find a way to work it out peacefully, but I don't expect I will, he thought as the Sampsons began to disappear in the haze.

There had been that first time when he had set out to kill on purpose. That was when his father had been murdered by the old Mexican Jose Conejo, and Scott had traveled across the border to get the job done, finding the cantina where the old bandit hung out. He had been fourteen years old.

Scott had stood beside the door of the cantina disguised as a young Mexican. He wore a loose white shirt and a broad colorful wrap around his waist. A serape of the same material was draped about his shoulders. The strings of a large sombrero were tied beneath his chin to hold the hat in place. As far as passersby could see, he was too young to enter such an establishment and stood waiting for someone who had gone inside.

Hidden beneath the serape was his father's shotgun, cocked and ready. Suddenly, the doors of the cantina were pushed open and Jose Conejo stepped out. Shifting the shotgun only slightly, Scott squeezed the trigger. The explosion rocked the street, and Conejo grabbed his belly, staggered for a moment, and went down, blood from the wound filling his hands. Scott, still holding the shotgun beneath the serape, turned and walked to the alley between the cantina and a hotel. When he was in the alley, he ran as though chased by a grizzly bear.

Beneath the loose-fitting disguise, he wore his own clothes and, quickly stripping down to those, he tossed the cotton pants, shirt, serape, and sombrero among some empty crates.

Scott was barely in the saddle when three men charged from the cantina with pistols drawn. They peered down the alley and gave chase. "There he goes!" one shouted in Spanish, and the three began to shoot. A bullet hit the piebald's saddle with a dull thud. Another spanked into the ground beneath the horse, exploding sand upward to sting its belly the horse began to buck, but Scott held on. A touch of his spur sent the piebald into a wild gallop behind the buildings, up another alley, and across the wide, dusty street.

He had scouted the village well and a few minutes later rode through the shallow waters of the Rio Grande.

The old bandit had killed his father, and yet Scott had suffered nightmares about the episode for several years. He had sworn never again to seek out a man to kill him. However, it often seemed to Scott that a collection of gunmen, fiddlefoots, and ne'er-do-wells had sought him out. But he found his oath easier to keep once he settled into the canyon, as it was an out of the way, lonely place. People seldom called, and he hadn't sought to make any close friends.

Chapter Four

For the next six weeks Scott kept a constant vigil, but the Sampsons did not call on him again. Maybe they'd been bluffing or had forgotten they'd made threats against him, he told himself, though he couldn't quite bring himself to believe it. Still, as the days passed and nothing happened, Scott began to relax.

They struck again when he least expected it. It was a quiet late afternoon, when the setting sun cast long shadows across the valley. Golden rode up to the barn and began to strip Big Red of his tack. About a half dozen bats floated above the barn, swooping low for insects from time to time. A wind from off the slopes rattled the dry leaves beneath the cottonwoods, a sound like the feet of mice scuttling across glass. In the distance the same wind stirred up dust devils on the flatlands.

Throwing the saddlebags over his shoulder and

carrying the Winchester in the crook of his arm, Scott started for the cabin. He was tired and worn out. His thoughts were on a bath and a hot supper. Suddenly, a bullet struck the corral pole six inches from his head, and splinters exploded against the side of his face. An instant later he heard the sound of the rifle, and then the echo reverberating back and forth across the canyon.

Scott tossed the saddlebags aside and hit the ground beneath the corral fence. The shot had come from the slope to his left. Now it was followed by another that chewed up the ground a yard or so from where Scott lay. Lying flat, he brought the rifle to his shoulder, ready for a shot as he studied the slope above the canyon wall.

The Sampsons have finally paid me a call, he thought to himself, as he wiped a hand down the side of his face and discovered the bed of small splinters. His hand came away bloody.

Nothing moved on the slope, but he knew that whoever had taken the shot was still up there. Maybe the ambusher was thinking that Scott would try again for the cabin.

Then the slight movement of a low bush caught his eye. Scott brought the rifle to his shoulder and put two quick shots into the bush. Sudden violent movement, and then a man clambered up and began to scramble wildly up the slope. Golden tracked his progress with more bullets as the man struggled toward a shallow ravine half way up the slope. He didn't want to kill him; maybe a good scare would do the trick.

The ravine ran parallel to the rim of the mountain,

and the would-be assassin threw himself over the edge. A moment later, Golden heard pounding hooves, and a horse and rider emerged from the ravine further on. The distance was too great to put a shot even close, so Golden lowered the rifle and pushed himself up. Apparently, only one Sampson had visited him this time. Still, he knew there would be another. And next time, the whole family would probably come along.

After he ate, Scott sat before the cabin and enjoyed the cool evening air. He had a decision to make. Lighting up his pipe, which he seldom used, he considered his problem. Should he take the fight to the Sampsons? Or should he wait for them to come after him again? He didn't think much of the first alternative, but did he like the second any better? The next time a Sampson came calling he might not miss.

A mockingbird burst into song from a nearby tree. Usually, Scott found the sound striking, but on this night the bird's song had an eerie, lonesome sound. The shrill howl of a coyote floated in from the desert. Scott waited for its mate to answer but no answer came.

"I know how you must feel, fella," Scott muttered.

Remembering he was to drive his steers to the Denver market the next day, he rose, entered the cabin, and went to bed. He slept before he'd made any decision about the Sampsons.

The sun had barely crested the eastern horizon when Scott drove the steers from the canyon and headed directly into the sunrise for Denver. As usual in late summer, the chilled air foretold the coming of winter.

Even an October snow wasn't all that unusual, but October was days away yet. He'd have plenty of time to get the steers to market and get back before there was any chance of snow.

The ten steers he'd cut out weren't quite three years old, but Scott needed more money than he had at his disposal for supplies. He was also thinking of calling on Blake Lester and offering to buy a few more brood cows. Suddenly, a contrary steer darted away from the herd to the right, and Big Red, without any prompting from Scott, cut to the right and sent the steer back into the small group. And so it went for the next hour.

Well before the sooty air that hovered over Denver appeared, the Indians struck. Scott saw them sweeping in from the north and was stunned. There had been no Indian trouble in these parts for years, except for a few raids on farms and ranches from a scrawny collection of renegades. As they came into rifle range, Scott sent Big Red toward them, even as he heard the pop of their rifles, saw the smoke, and heard the soft whine as bullets cut the air.

Well out from the herd, Scott pulled the big horse up and waited for the Indians, expecting them to stop or pull up before him. They did neither. Instead, they continued shooting, whooping, and hollering even louder, the sounds reminiscent of a pack of dogs just spotting prey. Two spurts of dust gushed in front of Big Red. Scott Golden fought to control the horse as it began a frantic dance.

As he calmed his horse, Scott pulled the Winchester from its boot, pumped a shell into the chamber, and took aim at the leading Indian. He squeezed the trigger, and watched the Indian straighten up and fall backwards from his pony. Still, the others didn't stop, and Scott took aim a second time. Before he got the shot off, he recognized old Manaqui, the renegade Arapahoe, who had caused most of the trouble over the past ten years. Colorado Territory would rejoice if Scott managed to shoot the old Indian.

Scott squeezed off the shot, and saw the old Indian shudder and grab his pony's mane. Manaqui swerved the pony around and, slamming his heels to the pony's side, rode hard in the direction from which he had come. The other Indians also veered away, imitating their leader. As they hastily retreated, old Manaqui turned back and, raising his fist high, yelled angrily at Scott. He was too far away for Scott to understand what the old Indian said, but the threat was obvious.

"I just made myself another enemy," Scott muttered. "But what was I to do? Let him and his bunch run off with my steers?"

The small herd had scattered during the brief skirmish, and Scott had to round them up. When he was well on his way again, he glanced back. Two of Manaqui's party had returned for the brave Scott had dropped.

His steers brought a good price, and Scott left the buyer's office in good spirits, his run-in with old Manaqui's bunch forgotten for the time being. Lunch hour was well past and, stopping in the nearest cafe, he ordered coffee, a medium well T-bone steak, mashed potatoes, and side orders of lima beans and carrots. When he'd finished the meal, he walked outside and stretched. He thought of returning to the livery barn to fetch Big Red and ride immediately back to the ranch but, for some reason, he found himself feeling sociable, certainly a strange feeling for Scott Golden.

The Golden Nugget Saloon was next door, and Scott walked to the front of the saloon and peered in over the batwing doors. A cold wind from the Rockies swept down the street, brushing at his back, and Scott pushed the swinging doors open and stepped inside.

The bar was long and stretched the length of the back wall. The usual framed nude hung above the mirror behind the rows of bottles, like hundreds of others from Dodge City to San Francisco. Scott had been told that the same man had painted most of the nudes. Someone had painted a cloth over this nude's most private parts, and Scott wondered if the gentle ladies of Denver had had anything to do with it.

Scott looked the room over as he advanced to the bar. A few dust-covered cowboys sat around tables drinking and playing cards. More dedicated drinkers lined the bar. Scott found a vacant spot in the corner near the left end of the bar and waited for Dave Logan, the barkeep, to come for his order.

"The usual, Scott?" Logan asked, wiping the bar in front of Scott with a damp rag.

Logan was tall and thin. The white apron he wore wrapped twice around him. His hair, red and thinning, was sprinkled with gray. A bartender's smile usually wrinkled his features.

"The usual," Scott said.

"One sarsaparilla coming up."

"Maybe you should give the man milk, but better skim it first, barkeep," a voice from down the bar suggested. "Whole milk would be too rich for a man who drinks sarsaparilla." Snickers and a couple of loud laughs erupted from most of the men in the saloon. The man who had spoken roared loudest of all.

Scott glanced down the bar and recognized Blackie Sampson. He had forgotten just how big and brawny the youngest of the Sampsons was. His midnight-black hair glistened from some kind of grease, and two saloon girls each had an arm. The dark, handsome features that still wore a smile disclosed two rows of very white teeth. His black Texas hat was pushed to the back of his head, held in place by a string beneath his chin.

"The name's Blackie, Mr. Golden. Blackie Sampson."

"I know your name," Scott replied, forcing a smile, "and I thank you for your concern as to my drink, but I'll have what I ordered. Bring me my drink, Dave."

"Some skim milk, Logan," Blackie Sampson repeated.

"I didn't stop in looking for trouble, Blackie," Scott said, and this time there was no smile. "Now back off and let me enjoy my drink. Dave, set Blackie up with another of whatever he's drinking, on me."

Sampson studied Scott for a moment, apparently deciding he wasn't backing down. "Barkeep!" he said, slapping a hand on the bar, "bring the man some milk, and be quick about it!"

Dave Logan glanced at Scott and then back to

Sampson. "He has the drink he ordered," Logan finally said.

"I ordered the man some milk!" Sampson said, his voice unmistakably menacing.

"Coming up," Logan answered, and, unwilling to get mixed up in what was obviously brewing, exited the saloon by the door behind the bar. When he returned, he carried a glass of milk, which he placed on the bar before Scott.

"Enjoy your milk," said Sampson.

Scott considered the situation. Blackie intended to fight. Even if he drank the milk, other demands would be made until Scott was goaded into doing what Sampson wanted. Glancing in the mirror behind the bar, he saw the eyes of the men in the saloon studying him intently. If he backed down, he'd lose the respect of every man here, and the story would be spread far and wide.

Scott's hand subtly dropped to his six-gun and slipped the thong free. Stepping back from the bar, he turned to face Blackie Sampson.

Sampson stepped away from the bar as well, his hand poised above his own gun. "You ready for a fight, Golden?" he asked.

"If there's no other way out of this," Golden said, his voice almost a whisper.

Sampson's hand was a blur. Scott's draw was more deliberate but just as fast. Two explosions filled the saloon, but which man's gun went off first would never be known. Scott felt a pain like a mule kick in his left shoulder. Struggling to stay up, he glanced at Blackie Sampson. A widening blood stain moved quickly over Sampson's chest. A grotesque smile of pain and surprise twisted Blackie's face. The six-shooter dropped from his hand, sounding abnormally loud in the silent saloon. Then Blackie Sampson began to sink to the floor. As he went down, his hand helplessly grabbed at the bar to stop his fall.

Scott found himself unable to move as he stared at the crumpled figure of Blackie Sampson. Only vaguely did he hear the excited sounds that filled the Golden Nugget.

Dave Logan came from behind the bar and took a look at Scott's shoulder. "You're bleeding something bad, Scott," he said. "I better get you to a doctor." He took Scott's good arm and began to guide him toward the door.

They met the marshal coming in. His glance took in Scott's bloodied shoulder and the body of Blackie Sampson before the bar.

"What happened here, Logan?" he asked the barkeep.

"Sampson asked for it, Marshal. Forced Scott into a fight. Ask anybody."

A chorus of agreement came from the men in the saloon.

Marshal Bill Baron was a solidly built man with a reputation for enforcing the law. He wore a broad-brimmed, flat-crowned Stetson pulled down to within an inch of his eyes.

"You better get out of Denver, Golden," the marshal warned. "The rest of the Sampsons will be swarming all over this town soon enough." He turned to the two men who had flanked Blackie Sampson at the bar.

"Jim, you and Nathan get that body over to the undertaker." He turned back to Dave Logan. "Get Golden over to Doc Beard's office. When he's fixed up, put him on his horse and get him out of town. You stay out of Denver for awhile, Golden." The marshal stood for a moment and gave Golden a hard look. Then he pushed the doors aside.

"Just a minute, Marshal," Scott said.

Marshal Baron stopped and turned back.

"Did you want something?" he asked.

"Just to let you know I'll be coming into town whenever I need to. I didn't start this, and I won't go without supplies because I was forced into a fight." Scott shook off Dave's hand, took out his neckerchief, and carefully packed it inside his shirt to cover the wound. He fought hard to keep from showing the pain he felt.

"When the Sampsons come, Dave, you tell 'em I didn't ask for this fight. If they ain't satisfied, tell 'em I said they know where to find me."

As Scott rode west along Cherry Creek, people stopped to stare. Apparently, word had already spread that he'd killed Blackie Sampson.

Facing the warm sun, Scott headed for the canyon, hoping he wouldn't run afoul of old Manaqui and his bunch on the return trip. He was far from happy about the gunfight with Blackie Sampson. Of course, he'd rather be in his position than Blackie Sampson's, he thought to himself. But he hated killing, and he'd managed to avoid having a hand in it since he'd come to the canyon.

The last one, the one before Blackie Sampson, had happened in the Dakota Territory. Deadwood, to be exact.

He had ridden into Deadwood to buy supplies, intending to ride south again before winter set in. He topped a slight ridge, pulled the dun he rode up, and looked down at the rugged little town, shifting in the saddle to ease the strain on his seat. He was close enough to read a few of the larger signs, and saw two saloons, a hotel, and a cafe. There were other buildings that looked like commercial establishments, but their signs were too small for him to make out. The center of town was surrounded by a couple dozen dwellings.

Pulling up before a livery, Scott was given an eager greeting by the manager, a young man whose smile suggested he hadn't been too long at the job.

"Morning, sir, want me to take care of the horses?" he asked.

"Not sure how long I'll be staying, so I won't hand them over just yet. But I would like a bushel of oats just in case I pull out," Scott replied.

"Got no oats, but I got plenty of shelled corn," the man said.

"How much?"

"Fifty cents a bushel."

"I'll take a bushel then."

The liveryman returned with the corn, and Scott placed it in the packsaddle on the packhorse's back. His next stop was before the first of the cafes. He swung down and tied the dun and the packhorse to the hitch rail. Opening the bag of corn, he emptied some into two feedbags, and tied the bags on the heads of the two horses.

"I'm gonna go put my own feedbag on," he said to the horses, and entered the cafe. The place was a mere strip of a room between a saloon and a hardware store. A long counter with several stools ran along one wall. Tables were placed against the other wall, leaving barely enough room for a customer to squeeze between them and the stools. The cafe was empty, and Scott chose a stool at the far end of the counter that allowed him to see his horses outside.

"What'll you have?" a short rotund man asked, coming from the kitchen. The man's head was bald except for a thin rim of hair above his ears. He gave Scott a shy smile that conflicted with his size.

"Some pork chops with all the trimmings, if you got 'em."

"Coming up. Two pork chops, potatoes, and sliced tomatoes. How does that sound?

"Perfect," Scott replied.

The horses had finished their corn when Scott returned to the street. He relieved them of their feedbags, stored these again in the pack, and eyed the nearby saloon. As he wasn't a drinking man, Scott didn't particularly enjoy spending time in saloons, but if a man wanted information about a town, the best place was in a saloon. He headed for the swinging doors.

The saloon was darkly lit and had the smell of stale beer and sweat. An inch of sawdust covered the floor. Scott was aware of the aromas as he walked to the bar. Glancing at the painting behind the bar, he came to a sudden stop. The woman in the frame was half woman and half fish.

"A mermaid," the bartender said and laughed. "Does that to a lot of folks who wander in."

"Never heard of or saw such a thing," Scott said, and decided his mouth must have been hanging open.

"Don't think they exist," the bartender said, "except in man's imagination." The bartender was middle-aged, with a shock of brown hair laced with gray. "A drink?" he asked, giving Scott a welcoming smile.

"A little too early for me," Scott said. "Maybe later. I could do with a glass of water though."

"Coming up."

"Maybe you'd like a little one-on-one poker?" a voice from the back of the saloon asked.

Scott drank the water, and turned to face the voice. For a moment he thought he was looking at Doc Holiday, the man had taught him to shoot and play poker when they'd spent some time together in Cimarron. But this man wasn't as pale or thin as Doc. He did wear the same black suit, white shirt, and bow-string tie, but there was something counterfeit about the smile he flashed in Scott's direction, a smile that exposed even but discolored teeth. The gambler thought he'd spotted a sucker, Scott decided, and felt a sudden dislike so intense he was surprised.

"Don't know much about poker," Scott said, "but I could while away a little time, I guess."

"Well, come on back!" the man said, hardly hiding his delight. The gambler held out his hand as Scott approached. "The name's Duke Barlow," he said, as Scott took the smooth, slender hand and shook.

"Scott Golden."

"A little five card stud?" Duke Barlow asked.

"Might as well."

The man won the first three hands in rapid succession, so quick, in fact, that Scott's suspicions that he was a cheat seemed confirmed. During the next deal, Scott watched Barlow's hands carefully and could scarcely believe the facility of the man's fingers as he slipped a card from the bottom of the deck and flipped an ace to the table before him, making three aces he'd given himself.

"You took that last ace from the bottom of the deck," Scott said, dropping his hand to the butt of his six-gun.

The words were barely spoken when a small derringer seemed to sprout in the gambler's hand. Moving quickly to his left, Scott drew and fired, but not before the derringer exploded, sending a bullet so close to Scott's ear he heard the whistle of the passing lead.

Barlow dropped the derringer and grasped onto his chair. "You . . . You . . ." he managed before he dropped to the floor.

Scott looked down at the gambler, whose eyes stared vacantly at the ceiling. Scott felt the contents of his stomach begin to rise, and he headed toward the door. "I didn't mean to," he said as he passed the bartender.

"You had no choice. I'll tell that to the marshal," the barkeep said to Scott's back.

Scott had ridden west out of Deadwood. He'd heard

of the desolate Rocky mountains, home only to a few Indians and trappers. That had sounded like the ideal place to him, and he had hoped never to draw his gun against another man again.

Chapter Five

Scott Golden arrived at his ranch feeling weak and grateful. Blackie Sampson had obviously fired at Scott's heart. His aim had been only inches off.

Scott guided his steed into the corral. Favoring his wounded shoulder, he unsaddled Big Red and stored the saddle in the tack room. Next, he ripped a strip from a gunney sack and gave the horse a rubdown. He then turned him loose in the corral alongside the buckskin, which was nibbling at some loose hay.

Scott entered the cabin, added wood to the coals in the kitchen's iron stove, and put a pot of coffee on to boil. Some cornbread would go good with that coffee, he thought. He stirred up a pan, mostly one-handed, and slipped it into the oven. The coffeepot began to steam.

It wasn't much later that he heard a horse approaching. Crossing to the door, he stepped outside and, with surprise and pleasure, watched Anne Barber step down from her black mare. A derby-type black English riding hat was pulled well down over her long auburn hair. She wore a green silk blouse and a split khaki skirt that reached to the top of slim black boots. Wrapping the horse's reins around the hitch rack near the cabin, she turned brown eyes flecked with yellow on Scott Golden.

"They told me in town you were wounded," she said, crossing to face Scott.

"Just a scratch," he murmured, nervous at her nearness and her close scrutiny.

She walked past him and entered the cabin. Scott could only follow. "I'll take a look at that shoulder," she said once inside. "The least I can do is apply a decent bandage. Where can I find some clean white cloth?"

"There's a partially ripped sheet in the top bureau drawer in the bedroom," he said. "I'll get it."

"No, you wait in the kitchen, and we'll need hot water."

Scott grudgingly did as he was told and sat at the kitchen table. Pleasure warmed him despite his misgivings as he listened to her footsteps and the sound of the bureau drawer pulled open. Oddly, the cabin seemed more comfortable. Certainly less empty.

A moment later she appeared with several strips from the old sheet. Indicating her familiarity with the arrangement in the kitchen, she found a pan and filled it with hot water from a kettle, a permanent fixture on every stove in the Territory.

"Take off your shirt," she said, placing the pan on the table.

"No . . . I . . ." he stuttered. "It wouldn't be proper."

"Don't be silly," she said and laughed. "I've seen a man's bare shoulders and chest before."

Barely breathing, Scott sat rigid as Anne unbuttoned his shirt and helped him slip his arms from the sleeves. Goose bumps peppered his skin where her fingers brushed him.

Gently, she removed the crude bandage Scott had fashioned and inspected the wound. "You were lucky," she said as she gently bathed the groove left by the bullet. "Six inches further in and down a little, and the bullet would have nicked your heart. I see it passed through. Did it hit anything other than flesh?"

"No. I guess that was luck as well," he replied. Nothing she said had really surprised him.

"Better luck than what happened to Blackie Sampson. This is already beginning to heal." She began to wrap the wound in the fresh bandage.

When she was finished Scott rose and went to the bedroom for a clean shirt. When he returned, she was sitting at the table. She had poured two cups of coffee and slices of the freshly baked cornbread lay on a plate before her.

"This is some of the best cornbread I ever tasted. Where would a man like you learn to cook?" She munched on the bread and took a sip of coffee.

Scott sat across from her, glad he had made the bread and even more happy that she seemed to be enjoying it. He thought she had never looked more beautiful than when sitting there at his kitchen table. She took another bite of bread and sipped more coffee.

"A man who lives alone learns to do a lot of things, hopefully some of them well," he said. Scott sipped his coffee and watched her eat, enjoying the fact that she seemed more at home than she'd ever seemed during her two previous visits.

"I came for another reason than seeing to your wound."

"Yeah?"

"The Sampsons were in town getting all liquored up. They've sworn to kill you. I told Marshal Baron I'd ride by on my way home and warn you they'd be coming."

"About what I expected, but thanks."

Anne Barber lifted her cup and finished the coffee. "I'll be going now. I'm a couple hours late already, and Papa will start to worry."

She rose and found her hat.

"I'll see you home," Scott said, rising.

She studied him for a moment. "Are you sure you want to ride with that wound?"

"I'm sure."

"All right then. I'll tidy up in here while you ready your horse."

Scott thought he'd give Big Red a rest, and had the buckskin saddled and ready when Anne came from the cabin.

"Let me help," he said, stepping to her side when she was ready to mount. When her foot was in the stirrup, he put his hands around her waist and lifted her into the saddle, despite the rippling of pain in his shoulder. She felt wonderfully light yet firm. Wondering at the boldness of his move, he climbed into his saddle and followed her along the stream and out of the valley.

It was nearly supper time when they arrived at the Barber ranch house. The two-story house was the finest Golden had ever seen. The roof, held up by four large columns, extended twenty feet over the front of the house to shade the porch. Above the entrance a balcony was balanced between two second-story windows. Everything was painted a glistening white. A hitch rack, also white, was well off to the side of the entrance, and Golden stepped down and tied the buckskin's reins. Stepping to the black mare's side, he intended to help Anne to the ground. However, she slid quickly to the ground before he was in position.

"You'll stay for supper," Anne said.

Scott was sorely tempted, but he had no desire to confront Dan Barber in front of his daughter. Today was not the time for that. The ride had tired him out, and a throbbing had developed in his shoulder.

"Thanks, but not today," he said.

"Next week?" she asked. "It seems strange inviting you to dinner when I know that the Sampsons are planning—" Anne paused, looked at the sky, then again faced him. "Everyone knows how the Sampsons operate. They'll bide their time and strike when it suits them best. They're snakes, but they're crafty snakes. There is really nothing you can do but wait."

Scott changed the subject. He didn't like seeing Anne upset. "Next week it is. What day?"

"Any day. You just saddle up and ride over. We'll have supper ready about six."

The week passed slowly for Scott, partly because he was kept idle by the wounded shoulder, and partly because he hadn't been able to get Anne Barber out of his thoughts. He couldn't get over how she'd come in and taken charge of him and his wounded shoulder. And she had been genuinely concerned for his safety when she'd warned him about the Sampsons.

Early in the following week, Tuesday to be exact, he saddled up Big Red and headed once again for the Barber ranch. Glancing at the sun, he guessed the time to be about three o'clock. He should arrive at the Barber ranch about five-thirty, he thought, if he let Big Red take his time.

Scott arrived at the Barber ranch house a little before dusk, well before the time Anne had said dinner would be ready. He again admired the large white house as he rode in. It looked even grander in the dappled sunlight of late afternoon, he decided. Pulling up before the white hitch rack, he stepped down and wrapped Big Red's reins about the pole.

Scott stopped for a moment to enjoy the sight of the big white house set against the high peaks of the Rockies, colored by the setting sun.

Streaks of red and gold climbed the western sky as the sun, a reddening disk, slipped toward the jagged peaks. From the closely cropped grass beneath Big Red's hooves, a cricket suddenly began to chirp. Soon a couple of his friends and neighbors began respond-

ing to his call. A bird flitted from an apple tree as
Scott stepped up to the tall door flanked by large windows.

He knocked, waited a couple of minutes, and then
knocked again. Footsteps sounded within, the door
swung open, and Anne Barber looked up at him.

"I decided to take you up on your invitation. You
did say any day, but if tonight isn't convenient,
I'll . . ."

"Tonight is fine. Come in." She stepped back, holding the door for him. "Dinner won't be served for
another thirty minutes. Perhaps you'd like a drink?"

"I would."

"Come this way. You can join Papa in the study. I
suspect he's having his drink about now."

She led the way across a spacious room, large
enough to hold Golden's small cabin two or three
times over. Groups of comfortably stuffed brown and
tan furniture were scattered about the vast expanse,
resting on thick carpet into which Scott's boots sank,
giving him the feeling he was walking through soft,
springy grass.

Anne opened a door, stepped back, and ushered
Golden through. Taking his arm, she led him toward
a fireplace in which coals glowed. Dan Barber sat in
an easy chair to the left of the fireplace.

"Papa, I'm sure you remember our new neighbor,"
Anne said, stopping before a settee slightly back from
the fireplace. "I've invited Mr. Golden for dinner."

"Pleased to see you again, sir," Scott said a bit un-
easily.

Dan Barber was sixty years old. His hair was thin and silky white, allowing his pink scalp to show through. As Barber rose, Golden put his height in the vicinity of a stout five-six or seven. Clear blue eyes were anchored in a face of light complexion and marred by surprisingly few signs of age. He wore a dark suit with matching vest, white shirt, and black string tie.

Nothing about the man suggested one who had wrested one of the biggest ranches in Colorado from the rocky mountain slopes and desert plains of Colorado Territory. Still, there was a presence about Barber that demanded respect. Golden also sensed an air of disapproval, aimed at himself.

"Mr. Golden," Barber said, and stepped forward to offer his hand.

"Sir," Scott replied, finding Barber's hand surprisingly hard and strong.

"Won't you have a drink?" Barber asked, seating himself again. "I'm having scotch myself."

"Whiskey, sir, if you have it."

"Certainly," Barber said, his tone suggesting the absurdity of Scott's having any doubt that there was whiskey in the house.

"I'll get it, Papa," Anne offered and moved to the small bar near the door.

"Sit there," Barber said, indicating the settee.

Scott sat, partially facing Barber.

As Anne prepared his drink, Scott's gaze met the hostile blue eyes of his host. Neither man spoke as they sized each other up.

"Here's your drink, Scott," Anne said, giving him aquarter-full glass of whiskey. "Another for you, Papa?" she asked.

"No, thank you."

"Then I'll see how far along Wang is with dinner."

Both men rose as Anne left the room. When again seated with drinks in hand, neither spoke for a long minute. Then Barber rose from his chair, reached into the wood box beside the fireplace, and placed two small logs on the red coals.

"Have you an interest in my daughter, Mr. Golden?" Barber asked, turning to face Scott.

Surprised at the blunt and sudden question, Scott could only stare at Barber for a moment. "I do admire her, sir," he said finally.

"How many cattle do you run in that valley of yours?"

"About a hundred, eventually," Scott replied. "The herd is building up good and steady now."

"No plans for more than a hundred?" Dan Barber asked, unable to hide his disdain at so small a number.

"Not enough grass," Scott replied, growing more and more irritated at the probing questions.

"I heard of your recent trouble in town," Barber observed. "Was it really necessary to kill Blackie Sampson?"

"He forced the fight. I was defending myself."

"I suppose you've been told the rest of the family will be coming for you," Barber said. "There are three other brothers as well as the old man. That old man is a mean, tough old bird, but his sons are everything to him. He won't stop until either you or he is six feet under."

"I can take care of myself, sir."

"I don't doubt that, but I wouldn't want to see my daughter mixed up in such a ruckus."

Scott wondered if such a ruckus was Barber's only concern, guessing that it wasn't. "I wouldn't want her involved, either," he replied, "but I can't control what the Sampsons do. Someone tried to ambush me last week. My strong feeling is that it was one of the Sampsons."

"So it's begun?"

"I suppose so."

"Then I'll ask that you not see Anne again. In fact, I've decided I'll send her to St. Louis to visit her mother's folks. I'll ask that you do nothing to keep her here."

Scott was surprised at the disappointment he felt at Barber's words. And he was just as surprised that Barber thought he had any influence with Anne. "Certainly she should go, if that's what she wants," he said.

"Dinner is ready," Anne announced, re-entering the room. She seemed oblivious to the tension that filled the air.

Thirty minutes from the valley Golden smelled smoke. Touching his heels to Big Red's sides, he asked the gelding for speed, and the horse responded with a fast gallop. A full moon turned the mesquite and cactus into silver sentinels, and small night animals scurried from beneath the horse's pounding hooves. Soon the mouth of the valley loomed before him, and Golden saw the smoldering ruins of his cabin, barn, and corrals. Everything had been burned to the ground.

Pulling Big Red up before the ruins, he sat and watched the last of the flames die out. Then he became aware of the silence in the valley, a silence he hadn't heard there since he'd brought cattle in. When he rode up the valley looking for his herd, he found only one left, a brindled longhorn cow that came out of the brushy enclaves only at night to feed, a cow he should have sold long ago.

"The Sampsons," he muttered as he descended from the house.

No doubt they had been on the slopes and watched him leave for the Barber place. Then they had come down immediately to begin their dirty work. Scott hurled curses in the direction of the Sampsons' ranch, then kicked at the dirt in frustration. All that he had worked so hard to build was gone.

"Well, there's no sense shouting in the wind." Scott patted Big Red and continued to speak in a low voice. "That won't do no good at all."

Golden's first thought was to start on their trail at once, but he decided against it. He would need supplies, and he knew he would find nothing he could use among the ashes of the cabin. The nearest place where he might get what he needed was the Barber ranch, but the Barbers would have been in bed hours before.

"We'll ride after them tomorrow," he said to the horse, his voice firm. "We both need to get some rest first."

Stripping the saddle from Big Red, he turned him loose to graze, knowing the horse wouldn't wander far. Then he thought of the buckskin that had been in the barn. He hoped the horse had gotten away. Placing the saddle against the trunk of a cottonwood, he approached the smoldering ashes of the barn and caught the smell of burnt meat. Amid the cinders lay the remains of the horse.

"I'll make 'em pay even more for this," he said to the carcass of the trusty horse. Returning to where he had dropped his saddle, he spread the saddle blanket and lay down, his head resting on the saddle. He lay for a long time thinking of the devastation around him, his anger settling into a steady and constant hate. Before I'm finished, they'll wish they'd never heard of me, he thought to himself.

Hours later, he fell into a fitful sleep.

Chapter Six

Golden stood in the Barber kitchen and watched Anne gather supplies and drop them into a large flour sack. A side of bacon, several cans of beans, and a small sack of flour went into the bag. Next, she stuffed various cooking and eating utensils into another bag.

"You said they headed south?" she asked as she worked.

"Trinidad, maybe even New Mexico, I expect. They'd have no trouble finding a buyer either place."

"Well, that should be enough to keep you for awhile," Anne said, indicating the provision sack on the floor. "You should be able to kill some meat along the way. That should help some."

Dan Barber came from the inner house carrying blankets and several boxes of cartridges. "These will fit that .44 you carry, as well as your rifle," he said, "and these are for your rifle." He dropped cartridges in the sack with the utensils, and gave Scott the blankets. "I've also sent for Carlos Gentry," he added. "He's the best tracker in these parts, and has his own grudge against the Sampsons."

"I thank you for the supplies, but I don't need anyone riding with me. They'd only get in the way when I come up on the Sampsons." Scott paused. "What's he got against them anyway?"

"Old Carlos had a homestead too close to a mining claim Jonathan Sampson owned. Sampson swore Carlos had settled on his claim. Sampson tried to run him off, and Carlos fought back. His wife and small son were killed in that fight. Carlos was severely wounded. I guess Sampson thought Carlos was dead as well, since he left him there. I found him and brought him here. He's worked for me ever since. He's been waiting for a chance at Sampson for years, but I always talked him out of trying it alone. Tonight I figure the time has come. At least, it'll be the two of you against the four Sampsons." Just then a knock sounded at the kitchen door.

"Come in, Carlos!" Barber called.

A lean, wiry man pushed the door open and stepped inside. His seamed face suggested an age well beyond sixty. Seeing Anne, he reached for his old hat and held it in his hands. "Ma'am," he said with a slight downward movement of his head.

"Carlos, this is Scott Golden," Barber said. "I'm afraid he thinks you might get in his way."

Carlos Gentry turned to face Scott. "If I do, you can tell me to return home, and I will."

Something about Gentry impressed Scott, maybe the steady gaze of the dark eyes, eyes that spoke of

determination and the discipline that comes only with
age. "I've changed my mind," Scott smiled and
reached for the old man's hand. "I hope you've got a
fast horse with some stay in him."

"A mustang, and mountain bred," Gentry replied.

They picked up the trail of the cattle a few miles
from the Golden ranch.

"They're heading south and being pushed hard,"
Gentry observed. "You reckon they're headed for the
stockyards in Trinidad?"

"That's what I've been thinking," Scott replied, "but
I'm not so sure anymore. On second thought, they
would know Trinidad would be the first place that
came to my mind. Why wouldn't they think I'd stop
off somewhere and wire the sheriff down there? No,
I think they'll find some place to hide the herd until
they can put their brand on them. Then in a few weeks
they'll push them on south."

"Well, there are plenty of places to hide such a
small herd among the canyons and foothills south of
here," Gentry said.

"We'll find them if you're as good a tracker as Dan
Barber said you were."

The trail was easy to follow. Either the Sampsons
weren't worried about being followed, or they felt
strong enough to take care of themselves if Golden
did catch up.

Scott pushed on hard. Despite the long strides of
Big Red, Gentry's bay stayed right with them.

Several times Gentry's eyes strayed to the left of

the trail. Finally, he swerved his mount and stayed there for several minutes, his eyes on the ground.

"Something strange," he said, rejoining Golden.

"Yeah?"

"I think we're dealing with more than just the Sampsons."

"How come?"

"Three riders are behind and pushing the herd." He indicated the prints of three horses put down over those of the cattle. "There are at least three more riders out there to keep them from cutting into the desert. If I remember rightly, there're just four of the Sampsons, but six sets of prints, at least."

Scott swung Big Red to the left and studied the outside sign for a moment. "Three riders is what I make out, too," he called to Gentry. "Makes six. The Sampsons recruited themselves some help from somewhere."

"Who could it be?" asked Gentry.

"No idea, but I intend on making them regret they joined up with that bunch."

By the time the sun was halfway down, they'd been in the saddle for a good six hours of hard riding. Golden kept studying the distances ahead, looking for dust from the herd. Once he thought he spotted something, but the dust turned out to be from a small herd of antelope, probably frightened by a prowling animal looking for a meal.

"Hey, look at this!" Gentry yelled and pulled up.

Golden steered the roan about and rode to where Gentry had pulled up.

"You find something?"

"See for yourself."

Glancing to where Gentry pointed, Golden saw the unshod tracks, and stabs of apprehension shot through him. "I make it about twenty," he said, "and no sign of children or squaws. That don't look good, but maybe they're just a hunting party. Anyway, there's been no trouble with the Arapahoe recently, as far as I know."

"Maybe ole Manaqui and his bunch," Gentry said. "Supposed to have raided a ranch down near Cimarron. Dan Barber was telling me about it a couple of days ago. Maybe he's come north looking to make trouble for folks up here."

"I've had a run-in with that old reprobate already," Scott said.

The unshod tracks fell in behind the herd, almost destroying any sign of the cattle, but leaving a well-marked trail.

"How long ago?" Golden asked, studying the unshod prints.

Gentry slid from his mount, sat on his heels, and studied several of the prints. Carefully, he laid his hand into one and felt the condition of the sand. "I'd say no more than two hours ago."

"Then we'd better be careful," Golden said. "Or they'll spot us."

"Wouldn't be surprised if they spotted us already," replied Gentry, studying the distance ahead. "Maybe laying in wait up there for us to catch up."

"You can turn back if you want," Scott said, glancing at Gentry to see how he would take the remark.

"You're mighty quick to question the courage of a man!" Gentry replied, giving Scott a stern look. "I ain't never run from an Injun fight and I don't aim to start now."

"Just giving you the chance to save your scalp if they decide to jump us."

"You worry about your scalp, sonny, and I'll worry about mine." Gentry touched a foot to the bay's side and sent him along the trail.

"Hold up!" shouted Scott.

Gentry pulled up. "You got some more suggestions about my scalp?" the old man asked.

"You just stay alongside me," Scott said. He sent Big Red to the right, into the edge of the trees that hugged the slopes of the foothills. "We should be near some cover if they decide to jump us." He indicated the large boulders they were passing and the frequent copses of scraggly ash and maple fed by the drainage from the slope.

"Maybe they'll be hiding themselves," Gentry grumbled. "If so, they'll be able to just reach out and scalp us before we know it." But he fell in beside Golden.

They rode in tandem for awhile, talking very little, but their eyes took in every detail of the landscape stretching out before them. Things were much too quiet, Scott decided. Nothing stirring, not even a bird among the low brush that skirted the slopes.

The sun, though low in the sky, had lost its coolness as they had ridden south. Drops of sweat popped out on Golden's face, and an occasional dribble ran from beneath his arms, getting colder as it crossed his ribs.

He had the distinct feeling that eyes followed their progress, though he had no idea of the source of such a premonition. Still, he was a man who had learned to trust his instincts, and they were telling him to ride careful and be alert. At the moment, he wished his instincts were a little more definite. Was the danger from the Sampsons or the Indians?

"Look back there," Gentry said suddenly.

Golden turned in his saddle and saw the rooster tail of dust. "Couldn't be more than one rider," he said.

"But who could it be?" asked Gentry.

"No idea, but we'll soon find out."

Scott turned Big Red into a patch of post oak, and Gentry followed. Both slipped rifles from the boots attached to their saddles and held them at ready.

Chapter Seven

"Papa, I'm going out for a ride," Anne Barber told her father, poking her head into the study where he sat with the ranch books before him.

"Be gone long, dear?" Barber asked.

"Maybe a few hours."

"Don't go too far."

Dan Barber was used to the long rides his daughter took most days. Anne rode as well as most men and could handle any horse on the ranch, though she preferred the small black mare he had given her as a Christmas present two years back. The mare was gentle and had speed and stamina to spare.

Nor was he concerned for her safety. No man would dare harm her, and not only because she was his daughter. Women, still scarce in the west, were given special protection, whether they were decent ladies or women of the night. Known outlaws, even the worst of the lot, would help string a man up for harming a woman.

Moving to the window, Barber watched his daughter ride out in the direction of Scott Golden's ranch. He had a moment of unease when he noted her direction, remembering what had just happened there. He frowned his displeasure. He felt she might not be safe there. Nor did he wish her to be around Scott Golden. Golden was everything he didn't want in a son-in-law. For instance, Barber had no idea what had gone on at the Golden ranch. He was penniless, and seemed to attract trouble.

"A bit like myself at that age," Barber grumbled to himself.

Anne Barber kept the mare at a steady pace. As her father suspected, her destination was the Golden ranch. She wanted to see how much work would be required to put the place back in order. Hardly admitting it to herself, she was afraid Scott Golden, his ranch destroyed, his cattle gone, might decide to ride off as suddenly as he had appeared the previous fall.

She knew nothing of his past, but Golden had intrigued her from the start. He was not what she would call a handsome man. But for whatever reason, the gaze of every woman, married or not, followed him when he passed. She was surprised at the thought and wondered if she was jealous. Nonsense, she said to herself.

His most arresting feature was his eyes. When Anne looked into those eyes, she sensed a strength she had felt in no other man except her father. There was mystery, too, a mystery that hinted at a steel honed on hardship, maybe even sorrow, and she wondered what had happened to the man to give him that quality.

Yet there was a suggestion of gentleness, too, if one looked deeper.

He was a puzzle she couldn't seem to grasp.

When she reached Golden's valley, she was startled at the burnt remains, even though she'd been expecting to see them. Anger rose within her, and she didn't fully understand why. Maybe her anger was roused by the simple fact that everything Golden had worked for lay in ruins.

Yet even amid the anger, a positive thought occurred. The first time she'd visited Golden with her father, she mentioned to Scott that he'd chosen the wrong place to build. The house should have been built on the slight knoll further up the canyon. As she studied the spot, the plan of the house came to her, a one-story affair, T-shaped, facing the entrance of the canyon. He'd need tall trees to provide shade in summer, and that would take a few years. Built from logs, the rustic appearance would suit the canyon perfectly.

A living room, study, and bedrooms would be in front, while the dining room and kitchen would be behind in the stem of the T. She saw it all in her mind and decided she would speak of it to Golden at the first chance.

For a moment she pictured herself presiding over such a house, and was startled by the diffusion of warmth that flowed through her. A tear unexpectedly slipped loose from her right eye and ran down her cheek.

"Maybe I should start being honest with myself," she said to the black mare. Anne wanted a life with Scott Golden, wanted it with a passion that frightened her. And Golden was now on a journey that could kill him.

Anne guided her horse out of the valley and found the cattle trail that led south. "We have to ride fast," she said to her horse as they began to follow the trail.

The black mare gave no resistance to Anne's commands. After a few hours of hard, steady riding with few rests, Anne spotted the dust clouds from two riders she could barely see.

"That must be them!" she shouted out loud and then suddenly reined her horse in. The young woman had been so intent on catching up with Scott and Carlos that she had given no thought to what she would say to them once she was actually facing the men.

She laughed to herself. Dad was right, she thought. Being stubborn can only get me in a lot of trouble. She spurred the mare on.

"Well, I'll be ... !" Golden said when he recognized the rider. Easing the dun from the oak brush, he blocked her way. Pulling up, Anne Barber smiled at him. The smile was brief, however.

"What are you doing here?" Golden asked angrily.

Anne was flustered for a moment. She said the first thing that popped into her mind. "I thought you might need help."

"Didn't you see the Indian sign? You want to get yourself killed or captured?"

"No, I saw no Indian sign."

"You'll have to take her back, Gentry," Golden said, his voice laced with anger and something a little more.

Anne's indecisiveness vanished. "If I decide to go back," she said, holding her voice even with some effort, "I'll go alone. You'll need Carlos with you."

"If? What do you mean, if?"

"I haven't made up my mind yet," she said defiantly. "You forget I can ride as well as either of you, and I can shoot. Seems to me you might appreciate another gun. Anyway, no one orders me around, not even my father. I thought you knew that."

Golden was too surprised to reply for the moment. Instead, he glared at her as he searched for something to say.

Carlos Gentry spoke softly to the young woman who had, along with her father, become the only family he had, filling a horrible emptiness left by the butchery of the Sampsons. "You shouldn't have come, Miss Anne." His voice became firm as he turned to Scott. "But she'll have to stay with us. She was lucky to get here alive. Manaqui and those renegades are out there. Miss Anne can't go ridin' back alone."

"That's why I want you to go with her!" Golden snapped.

"Well, you can't go after the Sampsons and Manaqui alone," Gentry said calmly. "By the time I get back, the Sampsons will have sold your cattle. They'll have triumphed again. In the Good Book, it says when your hands are on the plowshare you can't go lookin' back. Our hands are oft that plowshare."

Carlos Gentry's words left Scott confused and uncertain. Scowling, he scanned the horizon for several long moments before he responded, "I can sure see that I'm out-voted here!"

Frustrated, he took his anger out on Big Red, reining him about roughly and pointing him south. Big Red, unused to such treatment, suddenly humped his back and bucked, almost unseating Scott.

Anne almost laughed out loud at the rebuke from the horse and sent the black filly after Scott.

Carlos Gentry, shaking his head, followed. He understood what was happening between the two young people and knew that it boded well for their future.

"God in heaven, give them a future," he prayed in a whisper.

Chapter Eight

Jonathan Sampson was a man who seldom stayed in
one place, though his drifting was of his own choosing. Unrestrained by any moral scruple, he went out
of his way to enrich himself at the expense of others,
whether friend or foe. He had robbed, stolen, and even
murdered when someone stood between him and what
he wanted. He had fled Montana with his sons moments before vigilantes swooped down upon Virginia
City, rope in hand, to swing him and his sons from a
tree. A series of stage holdups in Wyoming were
traced to the Sampsons, holdups in which the drivers
and passengers had often been left behind as corpses.

Again he'd ridden south, finally settling in Colorado
near Denver. He had taught his sons well, he thought,
but he was beginning to question their talent, especially Boyd's. Boyd had insisted he be the one to slip
into the valley to ambush Golden, and Boyd had come
back empty-handed.

When that attempt had failed, the old man had decided the only way to revenge Blackie's death was a raid in force. He recruited the Sanchez brothers, Antonio, Juan, and Pedro, by offering to split Golden's herd with them. Watching from the slopes, they'd been prepared to strike when darkness fell. Then Golden had come from the house, saddled the red horse, and ridden out.

He'll come after the herd, and we can get him then, old Sampson had thought, and waved his rifle, the signal for the gang to descend into the canyon. Within minutes the cattle had been gathered and herded from the valley. Juan Sanchez and Champ Sampson stayed behind to torch the buildings. When flames lit the sky, they had ridden hard to catch up to the herd and the others.

They had pushed the small herd at the rate of twenty or more miles a day, and every man among them had orders to be on the lookout for Golden. When two days passed with no sign of pursuit, Jonathan Sampson had begun to worry. He had been positive Golden, no man to ask for help, would come alone. Had he misjudged the man? Had Golden ridden into Denver for help? Or maybe to the Barber ranch?

"Some dust back there, Pa," Boyd Sampson said, pulling his mount up beside that of his father.

Jonathan Sampson abruptly reined his horse to the right and away from the herd. Glancing back, he studied the barely visible plumes, and a look of concern passed over his bearded face. "A whole bunch of 'em," he said, "and only seven or eight miles back."

"A posse?" asked his son.

"I was thinking that, but maybe not. Golden ain't had time to ride into town, raise a posse, and ride back."

"Then who could it be?" asked Boyd a bit nervously.

"I ain't got the foggiest."

"Why don't I drop back and have a look at 'em?" Boyd suggested.

"You do that, but don't let them get a look at you. Then you ride like the devil and let us know what's up."

Boyd reined his mount about, and Jonathan Sampson watched as his eldest son became invisible, riding north into the dust the cattle threw up. Then he gave the signal to push the herd harder. We got another two days before we reach the canyon where we intend to hold these critters, he thought to himself.

Scott Golden remained confused. He was angry at Anne's refusal to return home. Yet something within him was pleased she hadn't. He thought of the sudden fire in her brown eyes and the angry blush that had transformed her face, and knew he had never seen a more beautiful woman. He had known few women and never one so fine. Still, he couldn't understand why her presence made him feel like a blithering idiot, especially when he tried to talk to her.

The sun drifted low into the western sky, and much of the brightness had faded from the day. The wind had settled and, to the east, a few heat shimmers danced above the mesquite and the occasional cactus.

Overhead, the circling of a lone buzzard seemed to follow their progress.

The shadows grew longer and faint fingers of pink reached out from a sun poised to sink behind the mountains. Still, there was nothing to indicate they might be coming up on the herd, nor the Indians for that matter.

"I haven't seen any dust from the herd all day," Anne said.

"Still too far ahead, I reckon," Scott said.

"We gonna catch up to 'em?" Gentry asked.

"Not tonight," Scott said. "There's a good spot for a camp a little farther on. We'll stop for the night and start out early in the morning. We should come up on them sometime during the day."

Dusk was falling when he reined Big Red up before the place he had told the others about. There was still sufficient light for Scott to see that neither the Sampsons nor the Indians had stopped off for water. Stepping down, he led Big Red through the brush. Anne and Gentry slid from their mounts and followed.

The seep, several feet in circumference and knee deep, was set well back beneath an overhang of rock. The trees and brush stopped short of the overhang, leaving a space the size of a large room, which at the moment was almost dark.

"Hold still a moment, and I'll get a fire going," Scott said to the others.

He took a tin of matches from the roan's saddlebag, and began to gather grass and dried sticks from among the fallen limbs beneath the trees. Anne and Gentry pitched in to help, and soon had fuel to last the night.

"I'll take care of the horses," Gentry said.

Golden sank to his knees in the darkness and scooped out a bowl a foot deep in the sand near the water to shield the fire from inquisitive eyes beyond the camp. Then he made a pile of the dried grass and smaller twigs and struck a match to it. Anne went to Big Red and returned with the sack in which she'd stuffed the supplies Golden had borrowed. Untying the strings from the top of both sacks, she took out bacon, flour, skillet, a small coffeepot, cups, a bone-handled cutting knife, and forks. Wiping a stone clean, she was already slicing bacon by the time Golden's fire was hot enough for cooking.

"You cook a mean meal, Miss Anne," Gentry said. "Did they teach you to fry bacon and make pan biscuits in that fancy school back east?"

"People in that fancy school back east wouldn't know a pan biscuit if they were to meet one head on," Anne replied, and laughed.

"You ain't saying your pa wasted his money sending you east?" Gentry said teasingly.

Scott had nothing to say, but he followed the conversation closely, his eyes covertly on Anne, who apparently didn't seem to notice he existed.

They sat cross-legged on the sand and ate slowly, enjoying the camp food, for the long ride had enriched their appetites. When they were finished, Anne collected the tin plates and other utensils, scrubbed them with sand, and rinsed them in water from the seep. Then they sat on rocks Gentry had rolled in for seats, and watched the fire burn down to red coals in the bottom of the pit, casting a faint red glow on their faces and on the rocky overhang above.

"I've a notion we ought to stand watch," Scott said to Gentry.

"Agreed," the old man replied.

"You take the first, and wake me at midnight."

"I'll take a turn as well," Anne insisted.

"I don't think so," Scott said and, for once, Anne kept quiet, uncertain as to why. Maybe it was the tone of voice in which Golden had spoken, as if he had the right to issue such an order to her.

Rising, Golden crossed to the spot where Gentry had stowed their gear. He returned with his bedroll and the roan's saddle blanket. "Noticed you had no bedding," he said to Anne, and dropped his own beside her.

"I can't take your bedroll," she protested.

Without reply, Scott stepped beyond the light. Spreading Big Red's saddle blanket on the sand, he lay down and rolled himself up in the blanket. The smell of horse sweat was strong, but it was an odor he was used to. Through barely open eyes he watched Anne, whose own eyes were on him. A few minutes later she untied the bedroll and spread it across the fire from Scott. Removing the small English riding hat she wore, she took a couple of clips from her hair and let it fall about her shoulders. The glow from the embers turned the auburn a deeper red, and Scott closed his eyes in an effort to shut off the feelings the sight of her aroused in him.

* * *

Golden sat on his heels just inside the trees that screened the camp, having been awakened by Gentry at midnight. Though Gentry had told him everything was quiet, Golden was uneasy and grew more so as time passed. *Too quiet*, he told himself repeatedly as, from time to time, he paced back and forth just inside the screen of trees, his eyes upon the starlit desert beyond. He had the feeling someone was out there watching him, and as dawn approached, he grew more and more uneasy. Still, nothing stirred . . . no bird announced the coming of day, and no rodent scurried through the nearby grass. Something out there somewhere kept them silent and still.

The sun half rimmed the horizon when they struck. As if they had risen from the earth, more than a dozen Indians suddenly sprouted from behind a row of small bushes, no more than fifty feet away. Their charge was silent, swift and fearsome.

"Indians!" Scott yelled, knowing Gentry would be instantly awake.

Scott rose to meet them. Taking aim at a huge brave who led the charge, Golden squeezed off a shot and the Indian stumbled and went down. They were upon him then before he could get off a second shot. Swinging the rifle butt first, he landed a blow to the head of the nearest, kneeing a second who came at him with a knife. Both Indians went down, but there were too many, and a half dozen charged past him into the brush.

Gentry was beside him then, furiously slashing with his bowie knife. Together they backed the four remaining Indians away. Suddenly remembering Anne

Barber, Scott took a final swing, smashing a face before him, and sprinted back into the trees. Anne was
backed against the cliff, a six-gun held with both
hands. As a group of Indians charged her, she fired.
One Indian stumbled and went down, but five more
were on her before she could get off a second shot.

Scott waded in among them, still swinging the rifle.
Wild with fury now, he slammed the rifle against the
head of the nearest Indian. Golden felt the jar clear to
his shoulders. The others turned on him; a rifle fired.
The blast was deafening, and Golden felt something
like hot fire sear his cheek. Losing his rifle, he found
the knife at his belt and fought furiously, slashing his
way toward an Indian who struggled with Anne. Two
braves blocked the way, and Golden had no choice
but to take them on. The warrior who fought with
Anne suddenly threw her across his shoulder and
charged through the brush.

"Anne!" Golden ran toward the fleeing warrior but
was tackled by one of the Indians, who quickly
jumped to his feet and smiled at his companions. The
smile vanished as a shot sounded and he crumpled to
the ground.

"Go after her!" Gentry shouted. "I'll take care of
these guys!"

Scott ran, madly pushing his way through brush and
limbs that snagged his clothes and grabbed at his face.
As he came from the trees, the Indian who carried
Anne was maybe thirty feet away, running hard into
the desert. Anne was still fighting, her fingernails leaving long red scratches across the brave's bare back.

Golden gathered his strength and charged after

them. It was a foot race, and the Indian was fast, though the weight and struggles of Anne slowed him some. Golden was rapidly gaining when suddenly Anne and the Indian dropped from view into a ravine.

When Golden topped the rim, the Indian was astride a pony. Anne was draped across the mount in front of her captor. As the Indian slapped heels to the pony, Scott launched himself, landing stomach-down on the horse's rump. Reaching out, he whipped an arm around the Indian's neck to keep from shooting head first over the horse. The impact almost unseated the Indian, who held on by grabbing the pony's mane. Already carrying a heavy load before Scott had landed on him, the pony stumbled and went down, tossing both Anne and the Indian over his head.

Scott, still belly down on the pony, felt his head brush a boulder as the horse went down. Struggling up, he looked around for Anne. She and the Indian lay unmoving a few feet from the thrashing horse. Scott crawled to where Anne lay, relieved when he saw the rise and fall of her breasts. He turned quickly to the Indian. The warrior's neck was broken.

Before lifting Anne to carry her back to camp, he examined her arms and legs and found nothing broken. Then, slipping an arm beneath her shoulders, he brought her against his chest. Anne's face was coated with sand, and he took a moment to brush it from her eyes and mouth.

When she opened her eyes, she gazed fearfully up at Golden, and then relief flooded her face. She said nothing for a moment, and then she began to cry, pressing her face tightly against his chest as sobs racked her body.

The sun beat directly down upon them, and no breath of air stirred in the ravine. But the building heat did not register with Scott. Despite the situation and the near capture of Anne by the savage, he had never felt so content in all his life.

"I see you folks are all right," Carlos Gentry said, peering down at them from the lip of the ravine.

Anne, hearing Gentry, tried to stifle her sobs, but had little success. Scott, his face red as a beet, felt compelled to explain why he stood there in a ravine with the woman in his arms, but no word crossed his lips.

"What of the Indians?" he finally asked.

"They're either dead or gone. Old Manaqui stayed away when the fighting started. He'll be back, though. After this he'll consider it his bounden duty to lift our scalps."

Old Manaqui, the renegade, as he was known among most whites in the Territory, was a man filled with hatred. Special circumstances might extend his view to someone beyond the tribe, but besides those special cases, anyone outside his tribe was an enemy. Of course, as contacts with whites increased, the worldview of most Indians had expanded. But Manaqui was a product of earlier times and gradually, not able to fit into the change in the west, found himself more and more an outcast even among his own people.

There had been a time when he had been looked upon as a great hunter and a greater warrior. In fact, he had almost been made a war chief. But the tribe elders had chosen Longbow instead, and Manaqui's isolation within his own people had begun.

He and Longbow had been close friends as they had grown to manhood. They had hunted and fished together. Then Manaqui had learned something about his friend about which he felt obliged to remain silent. He discovered Longbow was a coward.

The incident occurred when a young Ute warrior made a raid on the horse herd of Manaqui's father. Longbow was supposed to guard the herd while Manaqui built a fire on which to roast a rabbit they had snared. Moving some distance from the herd to keep from making them nervous about the fire, Manaqui was in the midst of his chore when he heard Longbow shout, a very loud shout which, to Manaqui, indicated something was wrong.

Jumping to his feet, he ran toward the herd. When he was almost upon them, he saw the source of Longbow's concern. Longbow had been surprised by the Ute, whose mission was to run off with the horses. Longbow's cry had alerted the Ute to his presence. Leaving the horses for the moment, he had confronted Longbow.

Obviously, the Ute now saw something in the eyes of Longbow Manaqui had never seen there and was now stalking the young Arapahoe. And Longbow was giving ground like a frightened animal. Then he turned and ran. Manaqui couldn't believe what was happening. He gave a fierce yell and charged the Ute, who turned and fled into the woods. Longbow then returned, pretending nothing untoward had happened.

But Manaqui, who never spoke of the incident, not even to Longbow, couldn't forget and lost all respect for his friend. Thereafter he avoided Longbow.

That episode of cowardice had begun Manaqui's estrangement from his own people. People, especially the women, among whom Longbow was a favorite, blamed Manaqui for slighting a friend and gave him contemptuous looks when he walked by.

The final straw had come when they were men, and the tribal elders selected Longbow as war chief. Manaqui knew there would come a time when the decision would be regretted, but he knew better than to speak his thoughts to anyone. They would credit such accusations to jealousy, as they always had in the past.

Manaqui was so bitter he did something unthinkable among Indians. He stole the horses of the war chief and quit the tribe, an act which made ever returning impossible. Gradually, Manaqui collected around him renegade warriors, not only from his own tribe but from others as well. There were Utes, Navajos from the south, and even Blackfoot from the far north.

All were filled with as much hate as Manaqui. Driven by their hate, the small band of renegades struck at Indians and whites alike. They raided ranches and farms, burning the buildings and killing, scalping, and raping. Soon they were known throughout the Territory and beyond.

Most of all, Manaqui had learned to hate whites, one white in particular. He had watched Scott Golden take charge of the canyon, once a favorite hideout of Manaqui's, and watched him bring in cattle and put up buildings. He had long thought of raiding the ranch and clearing the canyon, not only of the white man, but of cattle and buildings as well. But he also feared the man, knowing of his prowess with rifle and six-gun.

Then had come the raid Manaqui had led on the small herd the hated white man had been moving to the town called Denver. Manaqui's favorite, the young son of his sister, who had left the tribe to join Manaqui, had been shot and killed by the white man. Manaqui had a vision of his only sister, the sole person among his people who retained any positive feeling toward him, filled with grief as she wailed, whacked off her hair, and flayed her skin. With that vision in his head, Manaqui vowed to kill the white man and take his scalp.

Remembering Longbow and that incident now as he watched Scott Golden, the white man he hated above all others, Manaqui spat contemptuously and stared stonily at what was taking place before him. He saw the hated white man on guard, pacing back and forth before the trees. As dawn broke, he watched as his young warriors rose from the sand and charged.

Manaqui had to admit the white man had courage. Instead of retreating back into the trees, he brought his rifle up and shot a brave. Then the others were upon him, and he used the rifle butt to hold them off for a minute or so. Another white man arrived to help him. But the warriors were too many. While some kept the white men busy, others charged into the trees for the woman. A moment later, leaving the ground strewn with warriors, the white man he hated the most ran off among the trees himself.

Manaqui was content to sit on his pony and watch, a smile on his wrinkled face in anticipation of seeing a warrior emerge from the trees brandishing the white scalp. Then he saw Brown Water run from the trees with the woman over his shoulder, followed close behind by the white man. Manaqui was unable to see what happened in the ravine, but somehow he sensed that the battle would be lost.

He thought of charging the whites with his few remaining warriors, but he had already lost more men than he could afford if he was to continue his profitable way of life. Turning his pony about, he signaled the men with him to follow. Revenge upon the white man could wait, but sooner or later, it would come.

Boyd Sampson wove his way through the cover along the foot of the slopes. Soft sand beneath the dwarfed pine and ash deadened the sound of the horse's hooves and, not having to worry about being heard, Boyd rode north, hoping he might have the chance to kill Scott Golden. The thought brought a gleam of pleasure and anticipation to his dark eyes. From time to time, riding free of any growth, he could see the rising dust he'd been sent to check on.

Then, suddenly, the dust was no longer there. Reining his dappled gray up, he waited for the dust to reappear. Minutes passed. Had they stopped? He could think of no other explanation, but he dared not return to his father without the truth of who was back there and what their business was.

As the sun pushed west, the mountains' eastern slopes gradually turned darker, assuming the bluish tint of a bruise. The trees now cast long shadows into the desert, a tinge of lemon tainted the sky, and the tallest peaks promised to pierce the heart of the dying sun. The lowering sun and the altitude combined to turn the air chilly. Boyd Sampson shivered, and considered turning back again. What if there was a posse up ahead? What if he ran smack dab into them and was taken prisoner? There would be ranchers among them, and they'd slip a rope around his neck and swing him from the nearest tree for stealing Golden's herd.

As dusk settled over the land, he rode well back into the fringe of trees, and found a spot for a fireless camp. The posse, too, would camp, he told himself, justifying his decision. Then well before daylight, he'd get close, look them over, and ride back to tell his pa what he'd found.

He had chosen a place behind a screen of trees that hugged the slopes, not expecting water. But a slight drip from beneath house-size red rocks formed a pool no bigger than a small pan. Spotting the water, Boyd slid from the saddle and let his horse have what little water there was. He quenched his own thirst from the stale water in his canteen. He decided not to unsaddle the gray, fearing he might have to leave in a hurry, but he did loosen the cinch. Tying the gray's reins to a nearby sapling, he took his bedroll from behind the saddle, spread it near the horse, and lay down.

The hoot of an owl in a nearby tree gave him an uneasy feeling, lessened a little by the gradual appearances of stars, which seemed to wink at him through the tops of the trees. Finally, he slept.

A sprinkling of rain drops woke him well before dawn and, gathering his bedroll, he tightened the gray's cinch and rode from the trees. To the east tiny fingers of rose climbed the sky.

He had traveled maybe a mile when the first shot rang out, so near that his first thought was that someone had shot at him.

Reining the gray sharply right, he pulled up under a pine and watched a swarm of Indians charge headlong into a grove of trees at the foot of a slope. A group of about the same number sat well back in the desert and watched. Boyd suddenly recognized the old renegade, Manaqui. Jonathan Sampson had sold Manaqui booze and rifles for as long as the Sampsons had been in the territory. A lone white man suddenly burst from the trees and met the Indians, emptying a bullet into one and using his rifle to club another. Before the rest of the Indians surrounded the man, Boyd recognized Scott Golden. Boyd watched as the Indians closed in, and he was certain no lone man could survive an attack of such overwhelming odds.

Gleeful and yet with some disappointment that he hadn't been the one to kill Golden, he turned the gray about, spurred the horse, and galloped south. He would enjoy telling his pa that Golden was dead, that there was nothing now to fear from the man whose cattle they had stolen and whose buildings they had burned down.

After a hard ride that left the gray spent, Boyd Sampson came up to the herd about noon.

"You took your time," old Jonathan grumbled. "Who was it?"

"Golden and I don't know how many others."

Jonathan Sampson stiffened.

"But you don't have to worry 'bout him," Boyd informed his father.

"Why not?"

"He's dead. Killed by some of old Manaqui's boys."

"Are you certain sure?"

"As sure as I am that I'm standing here talking to you. Saw it myself."

Jonathan Sampson smiled, showing uneven, tobacco stained teeth. "Old Manaqui will feel mighty proud wearing Scott Golden's scalp at his belt. That was one white man he hated above all others. I wouldn't mind having that handsome head of hair myself. Reckon that old Indian would trade something for it? Maybe some of these here cattle?"

Boyd Sampson laughed. "More'n likely he'd want whiskey and a lot more rifles."

Chapter Nine

The rain the night before had washed the world clean. The sky, an indigo blue, was cloudless with nothing but space by which to measure its depth. The desert seemed to glow, and moisture still clung to the thorns of the cacti, though the time was coming on to noon. The usually dry air felt moist and chilled, and Scott felt the first breath of fall. Soon the aspen on the high slopes would begin to change, first great patches of yellow, then burnt orange and red. And snow, great banks of snow would fill the ravines and high valleys.

"We're pulling up on them," Golden remarked, indicating the slight column of dust ahead stirred up by the cattle, despite the rain.

"How close are we?" asked Anne.

"I'd say about two miles," Golden replied.

Golden was still not happy at having Anne along, but she had stubbornly refused to go back with Gentry. "Won't your father worry?" he'd asked.

"Yes, he sure will," she'd replied. "He'll set out to look for me, along with many of the hands from the ranch. That will certainly be a good thing for all of us."

Golden didn't say anything.

Gentry, who had scouted ahead, came from the trees. "They've stopped the herd to cook," he said, unbelievingly. "There's a little grass, and the cattle are bunched on that. Only one puncher to keep them from drifting."

Scott looked surprised as well. Another puzzle to add to the slow pace the drive had taken. Didn't they fear he would follow anymore? Or maybe that was what they were counting on. He reined Big Red up and studied the distance ahead. No sign of dust now.

"The time has come," he said.

"How're we going to do it?" asked Gentry.

"I want you to circle out and come up on them from the other side," explained Golden. "When you're in place, I want you to spook the herd back this way. If you can take out that puncher with your first shot, do it. That'll be our signal."

"Won't the two of you get trampled?"

"Don't worry about us. We'll take care of ourselves."

Scott watched Gentry ride well out into the desert to begin his circle. "Follow me," he said to Anne, and reined Big Red into the fringe of growth along the foothills.

Carefully, they worked their way through the trees, at times so thick the horses could barely push through. When they'd traveled a mile or so, Scott pulled Big

Red up and slid from the saddle. Stepping back to Anne's mare, he lifted a hand to help her down. Surprisingly, she smiled, accepting the help without a protest. "We'll leave the horses here," he told her, slipping his Winchester from its boot. "I don't suppose there'd be any use to ask you to stay. You'd be safe from the stampede here."

"You suppose right. I'm going with you," Anne replied, reaching for her own rifle.

"Follow me then, and be careful. I don't want to tip the Sampsons off that we're here till Carlos can stampede the cattle."

Pine needles and leaves from mountain ash layered the ground. Still damp, they became a silent pad on which to walk. Soon they caught the mingling smell of a campfire and coffee.

"We're still not close enough," Scott whispered.

Continuing on, he carefully pushed aside each limb, easing it back in place when both had passed through. They'd gone maybe another two hundred yards when they heard the sound of voices. The brush was too thick to see them, but the Sampsons were obviously very near.

Motioning for Anne to follow, he began to climb the mountain slope, reaching back to pull Anne up after him when the incline was steep. They reached a ledge a few feet wide, and Scott dropped behind a boulder, indicating to Anne to take a position beside him. From the ledge they had an unobstructed view of the puncher guarding the herd, and Scott recognized Juan Sanchez. The campfire was almost directly below, and gathered about it, coffee cups in their hands, were the four Sampsons with Antonio and Pedro Sanchez.

Juan Sanchez suddenly gave a shout, brought his rifle up, and fired. The cattle stirred nervously, and the men around the campfire scrambled wildly for their horses and swung astride, yanking their rifles from boots. Then the cattle began to run, continuing south rather than north as had been the plan. Ahead of the stampede, Scott saw Gentry desperately pushing his mount into the trees. Suddenly, he slumped over the horn, and Golden knew he'd been hit. Still, he was out of danger of being trampled.

The Sampson gang was in the clear now, racing away after the herd. Golden brought his rifle up, took careful aim at the nearest rider, and squeezed off a shot. The rider, knocked from his saddle, rolled for several feet as his horse galloped wildly after the others. Anne's rifle exploded beside him. She hit her man, but he managed to stay in the saddle. Both Scott and Anne managed to get off another shot each, but by then gang was out of range.

"Gotta get down to Carlos," Scott said, sliding down the slope and this time not waiting for Anne.

When he reached the old puncher, he sat slumped against a tree. Blood had already spread far beyond the hand the old man held over the chest wound.

"Let me help," Golden said, ripping the buttons from the shirt.

"Ain't no need, son," Gentry said, his eyes partly closed, the wrinkled face deathly pale.

Anne, rushing to the scene, knelt beside him. "Use this," she said, offering Scott a small handkerchief.

He folded the handkerchief into a square and pressed it to the wound, stopping the flow of blood for the moment.

Beside him, Anne had shed her blouse. "Bind him with these," she said, tearing strips from the blouse.

Meanwhile, Carlos Gentry had ceased to breathe.

"No use," Scott said. "He's gone."

Golden had known Carlos for only days, but during that brief time he'd developed a respect for the old man's courage and decency. Carlos Gentry had become a friend. As he gently stretched the body lengthwise upon the damp leaves, an anger such as he'd known only a few times during his life welled within him, and he silently vowed to avenge the old man's death.

With a strong stick, he dug out a shallow grave. Before he wrapped the body in a blanket from Gentry's bedroll, he removed the holster and six-gun and packed them in Big Red's saddlebag. He might need it and any extra cartridges later, considering what he had to do, he told himself.

Laying the body in the grave, he covered it over with leaves and loose dirt. Then, with Anne's help, he gathered stones and piled them the length of the grave to keep animals from disturbing the body. His final act was to remove the bay's saddle and set it astride the stones. Then he slapped the flank of the old man's horse, and watched the animal push through the trees to the desert beyond.

"He'll return to the ranch," Anne said, quietly trying to control the grief she felt for the wise, gentle friend who had always taken off his hat and addressed her as "Miss Anne," ever since she was a child.

"I guess we better bury the Sanchez boy, too," he said.

"But not near Carlos!" Anne protested.

"No, we'll dig him a hole out there where he fell."

For a long time Scott sat near Carlos Gentry's gave. He had felt such sadness only once before in his life . . . when he'd ridden out and discovered his father's body. Thinking of old Carlos and his father brought a hardness to Scott's face. Then the hardness vanished, replaced by something resembling tenderness.

Anne noted the change. Why had Gentry's death hit him so hard? Golden had known Gentry for only a few days. Had they connected so quickly? There had to be more to it than that, she told herself. Had Gentry's death reminded him of something in his past?

Not wanting to disturb him and feeling hungry, she built a small fire and made coffee and fried bacon, then made pan bread in the grease.

"Food!" she called to him when she was finished.

The sound of her voice brought him back from wherever he was, and he joined her by the fire. She handed him a tin plate, and they began to eat.

"I don't know a great deal about you," Anne said after a moment.

"You know enough," Scott replied, his voice gruff.

"I know you're a good cattleman, and you're fast with a gun."

"What would you like to know?" he asked, surprising himself.

"Where did you grow up?"

He didn't speak for a long moment or so. Then he began to talk. "My pa owned a ranch down near Presidio, Texas. Outlaws from across the border hit the ranch one day. Pa was killed trying to run them off."

So that was it, Anne thought to herself. Gentry's death had reminded him of his father's murder.

"How old were you?"

"Fourteen."

"Your mother?"

"She worked herself to death a long time before that."

"What happened to the ranch?"

"I decided to sell it. That's what Pa told me to do just before he died."

The wind made a sighing sound through the needles of the pines. From somewhere near, a meadow lark sang a few notes and was silent. Golden again began to talk.

"I took only a horse and saddle and Pa's six-gun and shotgun when I rode out. I decided to make Jose Conejo, Pa's killer, pay the same price. I rode to Mexico, found Conejo, and shot him with Pa's shotgun. I rode north again and worked on ranches a few days when my belly got too empty. Finally, I wound up in Cimarron, New Mexico Territory. I made a friend in Cimarron. You may have heard of him, Doc Holiday."

A brown squirrel dislodged a pinecone, which landed a few feet from where Golden sat. A couple of chipmunks skittered to the cone, searching for seeds, seemingly unaware of the humans. If Golden saw them, he paid them no mind.

"Doc Holiday took a liking to me. I'd played poker

before, but never like Doc could play. He taught me the skills of the game, and though I never made a killing like Doc frequently did, I managed to prosper. When a man wins steadily at poker, word gets around. He may be known as an honest man, but he'll soon find the games closed to him. Then unless he wants to go to work, he has to move on. I saddled up and drifted north again, finally ending up in Deadwood.

"Deadwood was a salty town full of salty people, and I had to kill a man, a gambler who was cheating. He drew a gun when I called him on it. I was more than sick of killing. I'd heard talk of life in the Rockies. I'd never spent time in mountains, but the talk had it out to be a lonely life. I decided that was exactly what I needed, and I rode west.

"I spent a lot of time in the mountains. I lived off the land and never found anything before that gave me the same kind of satisfaction. I think I relaxed and enjoyed life for the first time since Pa was shot. Still, I felt I should find something permanent and useful to do with my life, though since then I've often thought of returning to the high country. No land I ever saw appealed to me more, but I left the mountains and came down to Denver. I spent some time there, but stayed away from the tables. Finally, I drifted south and stumbled on my canyon.

"I homesteaded the canyon and bought a few head of cattle with the money I'd saved up. I guess you about know the rest."

Scott Golden had never exposed so much of himself to anyone before. He was far from sure as to why he had done so now, but somehow, as he'd talked he had the feeling she understood.

"What're you going to do now?" Anne asked.

"I'm going after the Sampsons. I can't let them get away with what they've done. I killed Blackie, but I had to or he would have killed me. They know that. But this is far from the first time they've stolen and killed. Killing comes easy to them. If I let them get away with this, they'll just choose another sucker, and there will never be an end. Besides, they killed Carlos."

His voice was soft but there was an unmistakable undercurrent, something deadly there. Rising, he began cleaning the cooking gear. When he was finished, he began packing up.

"You'll be one against the whole gang," she said. "You'll get yourself killed."

Looking at her, he thought he saw concern in her eyes. For him? He could hardly imagine it. He couldn't recall anyone who had cared about what happened to him since his father was murdered.

"I'm coming with you," she said.

"What about your father?"

"I expect he'll find me sooner or later."

Golden picked up a pebble and threw it at nothing in particular. A good man had just been killed. His murderers had to be pursued. But Anne Barber needed to be taken home where she would be safe. Still, at the point where they were a trip back might be as dangerous as chasing the Sampsons. Old Manaqui knew well that Dan Barber would pay a large sum of money to have his daughter returned.

"When your father does catch up with us, he'll probably accuse me of carrying you off and shoot me." Scott tried to sound lighthearted. But he didn't feel that way. He didn't feel that way at all.

Chapter Ten

Y ancey Sampson took Anne Barber's bullet. Entering just below the shoulder blade, it left a jagged, bleeding wound that sent spasms of pain shooting through his body. Enduring excruciating pain, he barely held himself in the saddle as he rode drag on the herd beside his brother Boyd. He tried to speak, possibly to ask for help, but the effort produced only a gurgle. Blood spilled from his mouth, and Yancey's grip on the saddle horn loosened. He fell from the saddle, hit the ground hard, and rolled a couple of feet. Yancey Sampson never moved again.

Seeing his brother fall, Boyd Sampson pulled up, jumped down, and knelt beside him. "Pa!" he yelled, "Yancey's done dead. I reckon that woman shot him!"

Jonathan Sampson rode back and stared down at his second son. He stayed in the saddle, his face reflecting a fleeting grief, a look Boyd Sampson had seen on his father's face only when he'd heard of Blackie's death.

"Drape him over his saddle and tie him on," the old man said. "We'll bury him when we get to the canyon." Turning his mount about, he rode back to his place alongside the herd.

They reached the small box canyon at mid-afternoon. Fed by springs, Elder Canyon was a perfect place to hold cattle, and the Sampsons had used it for that purpose many times before. The herd was turned into the opening gap before old Jonathan was aware someone else was already there.

A small herd of sheep were gathered in the very back of the canyon, surrounding the largest spring. A dog slunk near the sheep, keeping them bunched as the sheep drank. A single shepherd, staff in hand, stood several feet away facing the sheep, his back to the approaching cattle. Turning suddenly, he took in the cattle, and Jonathan Sampson who was riding toward him.

Removing his hat, he watched as Sampson approached. He was an elderly man dressed in a loose, hanging cotton shirt and trousers. His face was very brown and lined with deep, seamy wrinkles, like the surface of brown mud, recently wet, but now crisscrossed with dried cracks from a hot sun.

"What're you doing here?" demanded Sampson.

"No comprende, Señor," the old man replied.

"Get them sheep outta here and do it now!"

The old shepherd bowed and continued to smile. Sampson very deliberately drew his six-gun. Comprehension spread slowly over the face of the shepherd, and he tried to run past Sampson. Sampson spurred his mount after the old man. He put two shots into his head from no more than two or three yards away. The force of the bullets slammed the shepherd face down in the grass.

The dog, seeing his master down, ran to him and began to lick his face. Sampson raised his gun again and shot the dog.

"Get them sheep outta here!" Jonathan Sampson shouted as Antonio and Pedro Sanchez rode up. Before the Sanchez brothers began to move the sheep, they stared for a moment at the old shepherd's body.

Soon the sheep were gone and the cattle settled on the knee-length blue stem grass. Jonathan Sampson then glanced around and pointed to a sheltered spot under an overhanging rock. "That's a good place for a grave," he said, pointing to the spot. "We'll put Yancey there."

When Yancey Sampson's grave was properly covered with boulders, Jonathan Sampson sat beside the pile for several moments, his face drawn and determined. Rising, he turned to Boyd and Champ. "Come on," he said, motioning for them to follow. "We're going after Golden and the woman. You two stay with the cattle," he told Antonio and Pedro Sanchez.

"What about the old shepherd?" asked Pedro Sanchez.

"Let 'em lie. The buzzards and animals will take care of him," Jonathan said as he rode away.

Antonio and Pedro followed the Sampsons to the mouth of the canyon, drew up their mounts, and watched the three fade into the distance.

"That Golden won't be so easy to kill," Antonio

observed. "They'll be a long time getting that job done. Let's drive these cows on to Trinidad. We'll sell 'em ourselves."

"There'll be questions about the brand," Pedro reminded his brother.

"I know a man who won't ask nary a question," his brother replied.

Chapter Eleven

Scott Golden and Anne Barber rode south. Scott constantly scanned the desert side of the trail, thinking those ahead might decide to split up, with some turning east to launch a surprise attack. But deep in his heart he knew the Sampsons would always stick together, whatever the situation. He had long since become familiar with the prints left by their horses. All heavy men, they caused the prints to sink deep into the sand. Scott could follow those prints easily, and he would simply go wherever they went. There was the herd, too. They would always be close to the herd.

The high upcountry bordered by even higher mountains gave the fall morning a chill. But as the day continued, the sun warmed the air, and out in the desert heat waves soon quivered and danced as though they feared being thrust down upon the thorny forage. A few puffy thunderheads of various shapes and sizes drifted out of the northwest, seeming to scrape the mountain peaks. Their underbellies slowly grew darker, suggesting rain.

As they rode, a sense of danger crept into Golden's senses, the feeling more instinctive than from sure knowledge that something was wrong. Studying the desert, he saw nothing there that might explain the feeling, but old Manaqui was out there somewhere. And there was always the fringe of trees along the mountain slopes in which the old Indian might lie in ambush. He glanced at Anne to see how she was holding up. She seemed more preoccupied with the heat than any danger that might threaten them. Sighing, she wiped sweat from her forehead but kept her gaze on the trail ahead.

Scott wasn't totally taken by surprise when the Sampsons suddenly appeared from a thicket of pines and ash to block the trail, their rifles at the ready. His hand hovered over his six-gun, but with two rifles aimed at him and one at Anne, he couldn't risk drawing.

"Go ahead. Draw, Golden," Jonathan Sampson urged. "My aim is to make the two of you suffer for killing my boys, but we'll make it quick if you like."

They were sure to kill him. Golden's first urge was to try to take at least one with him. He might be able to kill the old man, and he would have taken the fight to them had Anne not been present. But she was, and with a rifle trained on her. He decided to wait and see what the future held. He placed his hands on the saddle horn and waited.

"Get down, Golden! The girlie too!" Jonathan Sampson ordered. Scott and Anne slowly dismounted.

"Now you get down, Champ, and get his guns. Better search him for something hidden, too, and get the filly's guns as well."

Champ Sampson tossed Golden's six-gun and rifle to his father, then searched Scott for a hidden gun. Finding none, he went to Anne and tossed her guns after Golden's. Then with a leering grin, he began his search of her body. His hands barely touched her before she stepped back and slapped him hard across the face. Champ Sampson swore and stepped hack.

"She's a sweet little tiger, ain't she, Champ?" Boyd Sampson yelled and laughed raucously.

Champ Sampson, face red with anger, lifted a hand to return the slap. Before he could deliver, Scott reached for the angry man's shoulder and whirled him around. They stood face to face for a moment, then Golden shot an uppercut to Sampson's chin. The blow seemed hardly to register with Champ Sampson. He merely smiled and came after Golden.

Golden, surprised the old man hadn't already interfered, slammed a fist into Sampson's belly. The blow failed to slow Sampson. Then a fist that seemed the size of a block of wood, and just as hard, slammed into Scott's cheek. The iron-like fist had been aimed at Scott's nose but he managed to shift his head slightly and the blow scraped his cheek. Still, the skin split and streaks of light shot through Scott's brain. He began to sink and grabbed for Big Red to hold himself up. The horse, already nervous, shied away and trotted into the desert.

Scott sensed rather than saw the kick coming. He tried to scramble away, but Champ Sampson's boot caught him in the side, lifting him off the ground. Scott gasped and grunted as pain, sharper than any he could remember, shot through him. Sampson grabbed the front of Scott's shirt and lifted him to a standing position. He drew his fist back for another blow, but the explosion from Jonathan Sampson's rifle stopped him.

"You did a fit job on him, Champ," the old man said. "But don't kill 'em yet. I want him to feel what I'm going to do to him."

"What you want me to do, Pa?"

"Bring 'em in here," the old man said, reining his horse around and entering the trees. "Boyd, you bring the gal."

"Pleasure, Pa," Boyd Sampson said and chuckled. When they were well into the trees, Boyd turned to old Jonathan. "Let me take care of her, Pa," he pleaded.

"Then have at her, boy," the old man said and relaxed to watch.

Boyd, who still held Anne about her waist, turned her to face him and brought his mouth down hard on her lips. He brought his hands to her cheeks and held her face against his despite her struggles. Stepping back suddenly, Anne curled her hand into a fist and struck Boyd Sampson a hard blow to the chin. Sampson's head snapped back from the blow, and he began to curse from surprise and humiliation. Jonathan and Champ Sampson threw their heads back and roared with laughter.

"Thought you could tame her, Boyd!" the old man shouted.

Infuriated by the laughter as well as the blow to his chin, Boyd reached for Anne and kissed her hard again. While still engaged in the kiss, she managed to get her teeth into Sampson's under lip. She put all the strength she could muster into her jaws as she brought her teeth together. Sampson yelled and lunged back, but Anne held on for a second as blood began to leak down both sides of Sampson's mouth. Then she let go and began to spit in disgust. Sampson glared at her as he wiped blood from his mouth. Hearing the continued laughing of Jonathan and Champ, he gave a furious roar, brought his fist up, and struck Anne a blow to the chin that lifted her feet from the ground momentarily. She was thrown backward several feet. Coming down on her back, she lay still as blood from her smashed chin ran down her neck and into her blouse.

Scott awoke to the sound of a sing-song, moronic voice, but he couldn't make out any words, only a low gutteral sound of despair. He fought to regain his senses and realized that he was standing against the trunk of a pine with his hands tied behind the tree. Anne lay a few feet away. From her waist up she was a bloody mess. Still, she wasn't dead, for the Sampsons had tied her hands behind her back.

Strings of red laced the sky. He had been unconscious for much of the night. He now had nightmarish memories of falling in and out of consciousness with the Sampsons beating and mocking him.

"Yancey, everyone says you got yer ma's eyes."

Jonathan Sampson sat before the remains of the night's fire. His words aimed at an indifferent dawn. "She was sure a pretty one, your ma. She never shoulda died."

Jonathan's back was to Golden, but it appeared that the old man wasn't wearing a gun. So far, so good. Champ and Boyd were sleeping on the other side of the fire, about ten feet away from their father. The old man's words didn't seem to be stirring them. The two sons were in deep sleep. Still, Scott was certain that Champ and Boyd slept with their guns nearby. If they awoke to the noise of their prisoners escaping, he and Anne would be dead within minutes.

But then, maybe a quick death would be merciful. They really stood no chance and he didn't want Anne beaten any more by the Sampsons, or possibly worse.

"Never shoulda died, never shoulda died."

Scott shook his head angrily, clearing his mind of such morbid thoughts. He had to think of some way to get Anne away from the Sampsons. And he had to move quickly.

He tried the leather that bound his hands and found a little slack. Had someone been careless when tying him up? Or had the fact that he was unconscious made them slipshod? He rubbed his wrists up and down, testing the give, but there was far too little. Straining his wrists outward, he put all his strength into the effort. There was maybe a little stretch to the leather, but far too little to slip his hands free. Now he felt the warm wetness of blood where the leather had ground into his skin. Wet leather will stretch, if only a little, he told himself, and he kept on twisting and straining at the leather.

"Say hello to yer ma for me, Yancey."

Scott's wrists now were rubbed completely raw. The leather had to be thoroughly soaked now, for he felt blood drip down into his palms. He mustered all his strength and felt the leather stretch. Then, holding his thumb against his little finger, he made his hands as slender as possible. He slipped his right hand free, then the left.

His eyes shifted to the horses that were grazing a long distance away. At least, it was a long distance for a man carrying an unconscious woman. And the one path to those horses would have him stepping over the sleeping Sampsons. The only escape, he decided was the slope behind them. They needed to vanish into the foothills.

"I buried her under the big cottonwood. She always liked that tree. No neighbors came. Neighbors never came. Didn't like me. Well, then, I say . . ."

Golden moved softly toward Anne and touched her arm gently as he crouched over her. Anne's eyes opened and Scott placed two fingers over her lips. Anne's eyes remained open, looking glazed and not completely comprehending.

Scott began to advance slowly in the direction of Jonathan Sampson. The old man continued his bizarre monologue. Golden wondered how much Jonathan had been drinking and whether Sampson's condition would help him to escape with Anne.

"I didn't mean to kill ya, woman. But ya was actin'

so ornery. Screamin' when I hit ya, it did somethin' to me inside I had—"

Scott's left arm whipped around Jonathan's mouth and his right fist crashed hard into the old man's face. Sampson slumped to the ground. Boyd and Champ stirred in their sleep but didn't wake. Scott inspected the elder Sampson for a weapon. All he could find was a knife. He slipped it in his belt and glanced toward the area where the two young Sampsons were sleeping. Trying to find a gun was too risky. He needed to get Anne out of there fast.

He turned toward the young woman and saw that she was on her knees, struggling to get up without the use of her arms. Scott reached Anne, cut the ropes that bound her wrists, then draped her over his right shoulder. He carried her into a narrow passage that led into the foothills, then began to run upwards through several snake-like twists and turns.

Scott, still weak and sore from the work-over by the Sampsons, felt his wind begin to go. Not only did he need rest, but he had to find a place where they would be safe while he tried to do something for Anne. He was no expert, but he had doctored a few wounds in his time, and he knew Anne's condition was serious.

The sound of dripping water stopped him. Scott followed the sound into a small cave where he lay Anne down, and found the drops coming from the cave's ceiling. Unknotting his neckerchief, he placed it under the water, then returned to Anne and began to bathe her wounds.

"Where are we?" Anne's weak voice startled him. He had been listening for the Sampsons.

Scott hastily summarized what had happened to them. He didn't try to sugarcoat anything.

"Are they following us?"

"I don't think so," Scott answered. "Old man Sampson was drunk. He'll probably have them wait a few hours before they come after us. They know this area pretty well. They'll probably try coming up over the slope. We can't stay here too long."

"I feel so weak."

"You've lost a lot of blood. We'll stay here long enough for the wounds to heal a bit. Next we'll—"

Anne had fallen asleep. Scott didn't bother to finish the sentence. "I'm not really sure what we're gonna do next anyway," he said to himself.

The first job for Scott was to get himself and Anne out of the rocky prison. From where they were, the Sampsons could shoot down at him, and with only the knife, Scott would stand no chance against them.

Anne was only semi-conscious when he carried her from the small cave. Choosing the lowest portion of the wall, he began stacking rocks against the side. Soon he had a bench a few feet high. Then, lifting Anne, he climbed onto the shaky stand and eased her onto the ledge above, and swung himself up after her. Taking a moment to survey the surroundings, he gazed up at the tall peaks covered with fir and aspen, the latter's leaves faintly tinted with yellow and shimmering in the wind.

Despite the mess he was in, Golden remembered those years he had spent in the mountains and suddenly felt at home. If the Sampsons pursued them, and he knew they would, he would give them the chase of their lives. Lifting Anne, he walked rapidly toward the mouth of a small canyon a hundred yards away. Alder and some sort of scrubby oak grew so thick there, he had to push his way through.

The canyon gave way to a plateau with undulating grass that dipped into shallow ravines here and there. A few soapstone boulders, rounded and smoothed by wind and rain, showed through the grass. Like the backs of huge, half-buried gray turtles, he thought. The wind suddenly touched down and turned the grass into waves. Golden had seen the vast grass that covered the plains of Kansas, and though he was now reminded of those, the grass here was only a pittance compared to the plains. There were a few ravines crisscrossing the slopes, cut deep by wind and flood, their red banks contrasting strangely with the green grass.

Taking advantage of whatever cover was available, Golden pushed steadily on, stopping only occasionally to get his breath and study his backtrail, all the while hoping that the Sampsons would give up. He knew the wish grew out of desperation rather than any belief that such a thing might happen.

Where a small stream of cold water flowed from beneath some rocks, he stopped and eased Anne to the ground. Examining her face, he found the bleeding had completely stopped. Again, he used the neckerchief to swab her wounds. The process brought her back to full consciousness.

With cupped hands he brought her a drink of water. "That tastes so good," she said.

"I wish we could get you into Denver. You could use some doctoring."

"Who needs to go to Denver with a doctor like you around?"

"Just repaying a favor," Scott said. He lifted Anne into his arms again and went north, heading for what would eventually be familiar ground for him.

The rough terrain made for slow going. Carrying Anne slowed him down as well. On the second day her bruised face began to turn ugly, turning a dark red, and she became feverish.

He knew he had to get food into her if she were going to live. In one of the lower canyons a sage hen suddenly fluttered near his feet. Laying Anne gently on the grass, he gave chase. That night, he carefully fed her small portions of meat. After the first taste, she ate hungrily, though it was apparent that her jaw ached. He fed himself on half of the meat and, clumsily wrapping the rest in leaves, he stuffed it into a pocket. There would be meat to feed her for a couple of days, at least.

He began to recognize the territory and knew Denver to be somewhere to the northeast. Anne remained very weak and despite her joke he wished that he could get her to a doctor. He strode rapidly down the slope toward the desert plain below. Making the foothills, he stopped to rest in a saddleback. He first placed Anne on some grass and then stretched himself out to rest briefly.

From where he lay he had a clear view of the terrain for several miles, and his eyes traveled carefully from left to right. Then he saw the riders. At first, he thought they might be cowboys gathering a herd, for ranchers occasionally let their cattle graze the sparse grass along the foothills. He sat up and, crouching among some low brush, watched as they came closer. If they turned out to be a cattle outfit, he would try to signal them. Surely they'd loan him a horse.

Long before they came abreast of where he crouched, Scott recognized the riders as Indian. Three white men rode among them. More cautious than ever now, he remained out of sight until they were below him. Though they were still three hundred yards away, he recognized the renegade Manaqui and the Sampsons. Scott continued to watch as they pulled up and studied the slopes.

The very worst seemed to have happened, and Scott's disappointment was great, for against such a combination, he would have no chance of getting Anne to Denver. With the Indians to track him down for the Sampsons, he would have a hard time standing a chance against them even in the mountains. Easing back among the bushes, he lifted Anne and headed back into the mountains.

He had one advantage over them, however. He now knew where he would go. Had Anne's condition not been so critical, he might have felt relief. He imagined her enjoying the isolation of those high peaks with him, and was thrilled by such a prospect.

Scott fed Anne on broth from a rabbit and then watched as she nibbled meat from the leg. "What happened back in the Sampson camp?" He sensed that she was feeling better and wanted to talk.

"Boyd Sampson came after me," she said, the memory obviously still scary for her. "I fought, giving him a blow on the chin that made him even worse. He forced me to kiss him, and I must have bit through his lip or come close. He knocked me out then, and I don't know what happened after that." She paused and gave him a smile. "Except that you have carried me a long way."

She chewed slowly on her food for a moment and then continued. "I wonder where my father is? He would have been worried when I didn't return. Where could he be?"

"Maybe he found out what happened and is somewhere back there," Scott said. "I hope he brought his whole outfit along. We could sure use their help. We not only have the Sampsons after us, we have old Manaqui back there as well. Think you can walk?" he asked.

"I can try." She weakly pushed herself up.

Scott eased her down again. "Why don't we wait till morning?" he said. He smiled bravely to cover up his growing apprehension. He knew they needed a miracle, and fast.

Chapter Twelve

Manaqui tolerated Jonathan Sampson and his sons. He didn't hate the Sampsons; he didn't consider them worthy of that. But he did despise them. Even as a renegade, Manaqui set and met certain standards. He respected the men who left their tribes to join his own small band. He allowed no fighting among them, and he expelled from the band any brave who stole from his companions. Naturally, he never mentioned the fact that he had done the same himself at least once.

He despised the unhampered greed that motivated most of what Sampson and his bunch of grown cubs did. He despised their lack of discipline in everything but their appetite for gain. When they saw something they wanted, they went after it with a single-mindedness that astonished the old Indian.

Manaqui was sure that, given the chance, the old man or any of the cubs would gun him or anyone else for something as minor as a cud of chaw if they felt a craving for chewing tobacco and had none themselves at the moment.

Manaqui had no choice but to put up with the Sampsons, however. They were his source for rifles, a constant need, since his young braves knew little about how to care for such a complicated weapon and used them up almost as fast as Manaqui could steal cattle with which to pay for them. Manaqui had seen weapons blow up in the faces of warriors because the barrels were clogged with mud. Often the braves lazily stuck the guns barrel-first into the ground to use as props. He had seen them blinded, or else scarred for life.

He needed the old man even more as a source of ammunition. No white man, other than a man filled with greed, would sell rifle cartridges to a renegade like Manaqui. There was always the possibility that those bullets would be the cause of his death, or the death of other whites, in a sudden raid on a town or a ranch. Manaqui needed Sampson for still another reason. He readily took possession of stolen cattle, or anything else of value, as payment on the rifles and ammunition. Manaqui knew the old white man cheated him outrageously, but he allowed it, knowing no other source was available.

Manaqui's relationship with the Sampsons, tenuous though it might be, was sufficient for him to join them on their hunt for Scott Golden, that white man Manaqui hated above all others. He had another reason as well. Half of his small band had been either killed or seriously wounded in the last fight with Golden. Joining up with the Sampsons would mean he could easily survive until he recruited more discontented braves from the various tribes.

Having already given much thought to such a connection, Manaqui was ready with an answer when Jonathan Sampson approached him. That approach came about just after the Sampsons had allowed Scott Golden to escape into the mountains with the girl. He was waiting outside when the Sampsons came forth leading their horses and looking to pick up Golden's trail.

The Sampsons pulled up short when they spied the old Indian with his half dozen braves, fearful for a moment that they might be the object of an attack. But the old Indian smiled, showing mostly gum, which allowed the Sampsons to breathe a little easier.

"You lose white man and woman," Manaqui said, unable to completely hide his satisfaction at their failure.

"Don't worry, we'll find him again," the elder Sampson said, responding to the subtle taunt in Manaqui's face and voice.

"You track him in mountains?" Manaqui asked. "Plenty hard to track across rock."

"You don't like him either, do you, Manaqui?" Boyd Sampson asked.

"Kill my braves."

"Then why don't you join up with us?" asked Jonathan.

"Ten rifles?" asked the old Indian.

"The minute we get back from the mountains," Jonathan said.

"We join." The old Indian gummed a smile again.

Chapter Thirteen

When Anne had not returned by sundown, Dan Barber left his study and walked outside. He knew of Anne's frequent visits to Scott Golden's, and that worried him. He was sure Golden had plans to make Anne his wife, and he didn't like the idea. The man who married his daughter would someday come into much property and money. He would assume an important role in Colorado Territory. Somehow, he couldn't picture Scott Golden in that position.

He knew little of what attracted women to a man, but he was aware of a certain mystery that surrounded Golden, especially in the eyes of the young women of Denver and the surrounding ranches. And despite his dislike of Golden, Dan Barber was quite sure the man would never harm a woman, and he would let nothing happen to Anne when she was in his company. But that much one could say of any man.

He couldn't recall her ever being late for dinner and

when she hadn't returned by then, he walked down to the bunkhouse and called Bill Tremble, his foreman, outside.

"Anne hasn't returned," he said. "I'm worried about her."

Tremble was a steady cowhand who had worked for Dan Barber since he was twelve, starting as cook's helper during roundups and cattle drives. Working his way up, he was second in command by the time he was twenty, foreman at thirty.

Tremble had spent most of his life in a saddle, and his slightly bowed legs testified to that fact. He was short and wiry, but loomed large in the saddle when mounted and in charge of ranch chores or cattle drives.

There was no man alive whom Dan Barber trusted more.

"Where did she ride?" Tremble asked. Light from the open bunkhouse door caught his dark eyes and reflected his concern.

Barber hesitated, aware of the implication of what he had to say. "She didn't say, but she went in the direction of Golden's place."

"Been lots of trouble there," Tremble said.

Dan Barber nodded his head. "Think I'll ride over in that direction. It's not like her to be late for dinner. Get a couple of boys to ride with me, and have one of them saddle me a horse."

"I'll go myself."

"No, if something were to be wrong, I'd like you here to look after things. I'll meet them out front." Barber turned and walked back to the house.

"Right away, boss," Tremble said after him. "Dalton! Bliss! Get out here!"

When Barber came from the house dressed to ride, Bob Dalton and Curt Bliss stood beside mounts. One had saddled a big, rawboned gray for Barber. Bill Tremble stood nearby. Barber mounted the gray and led the way north.

"Send someone back, boss, if you need anything," Bill Tremble called after the riders.

Dan Barber knew what to expect when he reached the Golden place. Still, he was shocked at the destruction. Having worked so hard and for so long to develop his own place, he could think of nothing that offended him more than the destruction of a ranch.

A three-quarter moon hung low on the mountains, casting a clear silver light on the desolated valley. The smell of burnt logs was strong, the silence like a tomb. "Anne!" Barber called, knowing the call to be useless, and hearing his echo come back at him. Still, he called her again.

He had noticed the trail of the herd as he rode into the valley. Reining the gray about, he returned there and by the moonlight examined the tracks. Recognizing the prints of a particular horse was second nature to a cattleman, and Barber saw the prints of Anne's black pony heading south. She had followed Golden, Gentry, and the herd.

"Foolish girl," he muttered. "What could she be thinking of?" Turning to Dalton, he said, "I don't like this. You ride back to the ranch and tell Bill to send me more men. Curt and I will start after her. Bring back enough supplies to last for a week or so. Tell the men he sends to come armed and ride like the devil to catch up to us."

Barber and Bliss followed the tracks until the moon vainshed behind clouds. Not daring to go farther for fear of missing something, Barber pulled up beneath a cottonwood and stepped down. "We'll make a dry camp here," he said. "Maybe the others will catch up."

The others had not caught up when the moon reappeared and the two rode out again, pushing their horses hard. When they had been on the move for several hours, the condition of the horses became a concern.

"We'll have to stop and let them rest," Barber observed. "They need some graze, too. Maybe we can find some grass."

"There." Bliss pointed at a spot a few yards farther on. "That looks like pretty good grass to me."

Removing the saddles, each man gave his mount a rubdown with balls of dry grass. There was graze, but each Barber rider always carried a small bag of oats tied to his saddle when on long rides.

"We'll give 'em the oats first," Barber said, removing the feedbag from his saddle. He slipped the gray's nose into the feedbag and tied the strings over the horse's head. Bliss did the same, and the horses made short work of the oats, after which they were staked out to graze.

"I'll take the first watch," Barber said to Bliss. "You get some sleep."

Bliss studied the stars for a moment. "No more'n

three hours afore day," he said. "Wake me in a couple of hours."

Barber sat on his saddle and listened to the sounds of the night. The crunch of the grazing horses was the most prominent, but from the desert came the chattering barks of hunting coyotes, and overhead a breeze lightly flapped the leaves of a cottonwood.

He thought of his daughter and the night she was born. He had never felt so proud as when she had been placed in his arms by the midwife. Helping her learn to walk, ride, and even shoot had given him inestimable pleasure.

She had meant even more to him after her mother died. He remembered his loneliness when he sent her east to school. She had returned a young woman of independent spirit and mind. How lonely he had been while she was away, but what he'd felt then was nothing when compared to what he felt now, when he feared something might have happened to her.

The additional riders caught up the next day, creating an unofficial posse. Leading the posse was Jim Bender, one of the finest trackers in Colorado. Bender's father had been white, his mother Ute. A low, squat man with a round face and small but honest eyes, Bender had ridden with Barber for only three years, but Dan trusted him. Now Bender's eyes never left the trail as he rode.

Beside Barber rode Bill Tremble. Barber hadn't been surprised Tremble had come along. Tremble had helped raise Anne. He had stood by and watched as Barber taught his daughter to ride and shoot. Barber was sure Tremble loved Anne as though she were his own.

"I left Hunter in charge," he'd said. "Thought you might need me here."

"I might, indeed," Barber had readily agreed.

The riders behind Barber and Tremble were Bob Dalton, Curt Bliss, and Andy Stoddard. All were good and dependable men, skillful with both six-shooters and rifles. That, Barber knew, was why Tremble had selected them.

They came first to the spot where Anne had joined Gentry and Golden. Bender's sharp eye sorted out the prints of their horses, indicating they had ridden on to the south.

Anger flared in Barber, turning his face red. Why had Golden not had sense enough to send the girl back? He should have known that riding the trail of cattle thieves was dangerous. Then he turned part of his anger upon Anne, knowing how stubborn she was. When she made up her mind, she did what she pleased, regardless of what others might say, and that included him. But he would hold Golden responsible if anything happened to her.

When they came upon the dead Indians, Bender dropped from his horse and looked the Indians over carefully. After a moment, he rose. "Renegade Arapahoe," he said.

"How do you know?" Barber asked.

"I know. Members of old Manaqui's bunch."

"How do you know they're Manaqui's men?"

"I know the looks. See their clothes. No woman to look after them. Those rifles, only old Manaqui has the wherewithall to buy guns like that. He gets them from Jonathan Sampson."

They moved slower now, checking every seep and spring as they followed the trail. In time, they found the fresh grave.

"I hate to disturb it," Barber said, trying to hold his voice steady, "but I have to know if that's Anne under those rocks."

Tremble stepped down and, lifting the rocks away, dug down to the body. "It's old Carlos," he said.

Barber was visibly relieved and yet regretful. "I sent him to his death," he said glumly.

"Who'd want to kill Carlos?" asked Curt Bliss.

"They must have caught up to the rustlers," Tremble said, covering the grave again.

The faces of all the men were grim, but only Bob Dalton spoke. "I liked that old man. I hope Golden saves a few of them rustlers for us," he said, giving thought to what was in the minds of all.

"Let's ride," ordered Barber. "We've got to save her if we can."

"Miss Barber was here," Bender said, pointing to the print of a small boot. Been a big fight here, too. Blood there. Maybe hers. Man in bad shape tied to that tree."

"But where did they go?" Dan Barber demanded, his voice a mixture of apprehension and anger.

"She was carried away," he said, following the jumbled prints to the narrow slit in the rear rock wall.

"How do you know?"

"Only a man's prints . . . big," Bender replied, pointing to the large tracks that led to the opening. "Miss Barber was hurt," he added, pointing to several drops of blood along the passageway.

"How do you know it's her that's hurt?"

"Blood there." He pointed to where Anne had lain. "Blood here." Now he pointed to the entrance into the passage.

"Well, let's get after them!" Barber ordered.

"If we go through there, we'll have to go on foot," Bender said, pointing to the narrow passage.

There were groans of protest from the cowboys. Cowboys protested doing anything that couldn't be done from the back of a horse.

"Isn't there another way around and into those mountains?" asked Dalton.

"Maybe," said Bender. "We'll make better time later if we can stay mounted and track them."

"You lead the way then," Barber said.

Chapter Fourteen

Golden had been in many dangerous situations before, but none equaled what he faced now. Chasing him were two implacable enemies, the Sampsons and Manaqui, the renegade Arapahoe.

Facing two such formidable foes was dangerous enough under the best of circumstances, but Anne, whom he needed to protect from them, was still not at her best. And Golden himself had suffered a severe beating at the hands of the Sampsons, suffering possible broken ribs and deep cuts and bruises to his face. His concern was not for himself, however, but for Anne.

Was he falling in love with her? He hoped not, for there was no possibility of a future together for them. They were too different. Anne was an educated women. She was used to all the comforts money could buy. Scott's wife, if he ever married, would have her hands full cooking, washing, and helping out on the ranch. He couldn't for the life of him see Anne in that role.

Yet whatever his feelings for her, he still had to protect her from the Sampsons, and he had little with which to do that. His only real weapon was the knife he had taken from Jonathan Sampson. The rest of his belongings were slim, indeed, consisting of a small tin of matches he always carried in his pocket and a small pocket knife the Sampsons had missed when they searched him. Not much with which to fight off the bunch that chased them. If only he had a gun . . . but worse than not having a gun was their lack of food. That worried Golden most of all.

They were steadily climbing to the northwest, through rougher and rougher terrain, aiming at an immense, tall peak that Golden knew. Just north of that peak lay the alpine valley in which Golden had spent his last year in the mountains, wintering there and surviving despite twelve-foot snow drifts and temperatures well below zero most of the time. If they could lose their pursuers and reach that valley with a little time before winter set in, he thought they might stand a chance of surviving.

But there would be much to do, and little time in which to do it. Winter snows often came early that high up, and he would have to find food to last them through the winter. They would need to have firewood as well, though Golden had left an ample supply of fuel in the cave when he left. He thought of the meager supply of matches in the tin and wondered if there would be enough to last the winter. They'd have to keep a fire burning constantly, as he had done before, but if the fire went out, there were others ways of starting it again. But there were more immediate problems to be faced here and now. Hunger, for one.

He couldn't remember the last time he had eaten, and he knew Anne had to be in even greater need of food. Passing through a small canyon, he spotted a patch of blueberries. They were past their prime this late in the fall, but a few berries remained. There was also sign that a bear had visited the berry patch recently.

He pointed the berries out to Anne and helped her to kneel. Hungrily, she began to pick berries, eating them as fast as she could. Scott followed her example, and they spent a precious ten minutes enjoying the sweet taste of the berries before Scott felt compelled to move on. But the few berries they had managed to eat did little to fill their empty bellies and ease the pangs of hunger, so Scott kept a lookout for something more.

At the end of the canyon, they were confronted by a slope that would have been a cinch for Golden, but which presented a problem when he was half-carrying Anne. Fortunately, the slope was heavily wooded. With an arm around Anne's waist, he reached for the limb of an evergreen and pulled, doing the same each time a tree or bush was near. Still, the going was slow and Scott, not knowing how near the Sampsons and Manaqui were, felt a touch of panic. If they were caught here in the open in the act of climbing, there would be little he could do. Not that there was that much he could do regardless of where they might be caught, for the Sampsons and the Indians would have guns.

Finally, they topped out on a spacious crest dotted with fir, and Scott let Anne sink to the grass for a rest. From the plateau of rock Scott had a clear view of their backtrail. Facing east, he studied the ravines and ridges for any sign of their pursuers. He soon spotted several dark specks that quickly became moving riders. They were four or five hours back, he speculated, and he congratulated himself momentarily on leaving so little sign for the old Indian, for Manaqui would be doing the tracking, no doubt. He didn't mention what he had seen to Anne, and after five more minutes of rest, he reached for her arm and helped her to her feet.

They were halfway across the crest when they rounded a fir and saw the grizzly. The bear was maybe fifty feet away and faced them over the half-eaten carcass of a small deer. Sensing their presence, he gave a gruff snort and rose upright to intimidate them.

Golden knew that bears were notoriously short-sighted but had an extraordinary sense of smell. Bears had grown to fear the smell of humans, and this bear, not much more than two years old and weighing no more than five hundred pounds, seemed ready to flee.

"Stay behind the tree," Golden cautioned Anne.

"What're you going to do?"

"I'm going to try to get us some of that meat."

"Won't he fight?"

"Maybe, but he looks nervous. Maybe I can scare him off."

Scott looked around and, seeing a fallen limb,

picked it up. The limb had several smaller branches and a few dead leaves. Holding the branch before him, Scott slowly closed in. The bear suddenly gave a loud roar and rose again to his hind legs. The claws of his forepaws, bloody from tearing at the deer, were extended. Though maybe a little small, he was still as tall as a man.

Scott kept walking, giving the limb a shake from time to time. The bear, becoming more agitated by the moment, was being pushed to action. When he dropped to four feet again, would he charge? Or would he retreat? Both were pertinent questions, and Scott wished he knew which before it was too late. Deciding not to leave the decision to the grizzly, Scott suddenly took the initiative.

Flinging the branch about wildly, Scott rushed the bear.

The grizzly came down on all fours and, with a frightened yelp, took off, looking back as he ran. He stopped about fifty yards off, where he continued to stare back at the man who was stealing his meal.

Golden grabbed the knife and cut out two of the finer portions of venison. Little effort was required to secure enough skin in which to wrap and carry the meat. When he was finished, he backed away.

"I've left you some," he called to the bear and then turned to find Anne watching him.

"That's thoughtful of you," she said and smiled.

They took a circuitous route across the crest away from the bear. But before they began their descent, they turned back for a look. The bear had returned to the remains of the deer and was busily at work, no longer aware of them.

When they stopped for the night, Golden used one of his precious matches to light a fire deep in an overhang of rock. The shelter was screened by a thick growth of birch and aspen, but he kept the fire small. A birch provided two small limbs that Scott whittled into a point sharp enough to pierce the two large chunks of venison.

They enjoyed the warmth as they sat beside the fire and ate. "I've never eaten anything so good," Anne commented between bites.

"Be better with a little salt," Golden replied.

"Then it would be too good to eat."

"I won't be gone long," Golden said after they had eaten. He went quietly out of the overhang and into the trees. When he emerged from cover, he paused and looked around, his ears tuned for any sound out of the ordinary. Nothing aroused his suspicions, and he glanced at the heavens. The moon had still to rise, but the stars were out and sparkled from a deep steel-blue sky.

He had been sure he liked his valley ranch and, at the time, thought he liked working his cattle. Now, standing here, staring into these starlit depths, with the broad vistas before him, he knew he had never really felt free on his ranch. The cattle had only tied him down, and the valley had been too close to towns and people. Here among some of the highest mountains in the world was his true home.

He thought of Anne Barber behind him. "When she's well and the danger over, I'll take her back," he whispered to the stars. "But I'll come back." Then suddenly the idea of being alone, even at the top of the world, lost a little of its luster. What if she decided she wanted to stay? The idea seemed preposterous, and he put the thought aside, for such would never happen, he knew.

Once again he surveyed his surroundings, searching for any foreign movement or sound. In the distance, far below, he heard the call of a coyote. Moments later came the answer of its mate. A few feet before him a mouse stirred the grass. Suddenly, an owl swooped down from a nearby tree. The mouse squealed once before the owl caught it and rose silently to the tree again.

When he returned, Golden got quite a surprise. The fire was a bed of red coals, graying at the edges, and Anne slept a few feet away. Snuggled in the bend of her arm was a bundle of fur.

"A dog!" he said, not realizing he spoke aloud.

"A puppy," Anne said sleepily, pushing up on her elbow and massaging the puppy's bony head, pulling at his upright ears.

"Where did he come from?"

"I don't know. Maybe belonged to Indians and got lost. He wandered in a few minutes ago."

"Indians don't lose puppies," he said.

"Well, maybe he ran away then. Anyway, I'm not going to leave him behind." Scott sighed. Another mouth to feed, he thought. But he would never intentionally erase the contentment the puppy seemed to have brought her.

Manaqui led the six Indians and three white men into the mountains. He was familiar enough with the lay of the foothills to know about where the crevice through which Golden had escaped came out. He picked up the trail at once, and felt a grim satisfaction that Golden might be at his mercy soon. He gave no thought to what the white men might do, though obviously they had some ideas of their own about Golden. But the Sampsons, whatever they might want to do, wouldn't stand a chance once Manaqui got his hands on the man. He intended to peel the hide inch by inch from Golden, and then stake him in an ant bed, the big, red stinging kind. He'd do the same to the Sampsons if they tried to interfere.

Golden knew something about hiding a trail, and tracking him wasn't easy, Manaqui thought to himself. But Manaqui's old eyes were still sharp. His sense of smell remained even stronger and he frequently slid from his pony to sniff a rock or study a bit of sand that looked disturbed.

"Look at that old fool," Boyd Sampson muttered to his brother Champ, their horses side by side. "You'd think he was a hound dog, sniveling around like that. We oughta just spread out and search."

"I expect you're right," answered Champ. "That fella's hurt something bad after the pounding we gave him, and the girl's gonna be worse. I expect the two of them just crawled off into the rocks and died."

"I'd surely like to see that," Boyd said and snickered.

Jonathan Sampson, hearing their voices but not understanding what was said, turned and gave them a stern look. Despite the way he felt about them, he'd become disenchanted with them over the past couple of days. They had remained boys instead of maturing into men. He wondered what would happen to them after he was gone.

The slow pace while the old Indian checked out every rock and bush went on for several hours, and the Sampsons became more and more bored and frustrated by the slow progress.

Suddenly, Manaqui stopped, turned his pony about, and stared intently back the way they had come. "You hear something?" Jonathan Sampson asked.

"Somebody come," replied the old Indian, his eyes and ears tuned to their backtrail.

"Boyd, you drop back and see who it is," Jonathan ordered.

"But, Pa . . ."

"Do as I say," Jonathan ordered again. "We can't have somebody sneaking up behind us at a time like this. Now git!"

Boyd was careful on that ride, taking every precaution by keeping his mount at a slow pace, sometimes even walking and leading the horse. At times, he felt sure he could feel unknown eyes, and nervous sweat popped out under his arms, and the dampness seeped through his clothes. This sweat mixed with the odors of previous sweats and the foul odor drifted along behind him. Finally, he came out on a small plateau from which he could see eastward for many miles, and what he saw startled him.

He counted six men, their sizes ant-like as they

climbed, he recognized the one in front. Bender, the half-breed, was well ahead of the others. Obviously, they were following the sign left by Boyd's own party. He crept hurriedly to where he'd left his horse and mounted quickly. He wondered what his old man would say about what he would report.

Jonathan was as fidgety as a tomcat's tail in a room full of rockers as he followed Manaqui and waited for Boyd's return. Maybe Golden had got word to Marshal Baron somehow, and the marshal had come with a posse. What was to be done then? If the marshal caught him with old Manaqui, he might very well put two and two together and come up with four, and Jonathan Sampson's whole setup would be ruined if the marshal found out he was the source of the old Indian's rifles.

"It's that woman's pa," Boyd reported when he finally returned.

"You sure? How close did you get?"

"Close enough to recognize Bender, that half-breed who works for Barber."

"How many?"

"Six, I think."

"Did they see you?"

Boyd gave his father a contemptuous look. "I didn't come within a mile of them, Pa. I just stood on a high-up ledge and watched them trying to find their way up here. They're hours behind. We ain't got nothing to worry about."

Reassured, Jonathan returned his attention to Manaqui. The old Indian, who had dropped from his pony to sniff more sand, grunted and climbed aboard, picking up the slow quest once again. Jonathan was aware of the contempt in which he was held by the old Indian. Well, he needed the old fool now. When Golden was taken care of, maybe Jonathan would see just what the old Indian was made of.

By the time night fell, everyone was done in, including the horses. Jonathan hesitated to build a fire, though the mountain cold seeped through his clothes and penetrated to his very bones. He knew very well that Golden was capable of doubling back and would see the flames. Then he heard old Manaqui give the order, and soon a fire was throwing dancing shadows of the kneeling, blanket-wrapped Indians against the trees. Jonathan thought of hunkering down among the Indians and then reconsidered. He wasn't friends with the renegades and never would be.

An additional fire would do no more to attract Golden, Jonathan decided, and he ordered Champ to gather wood and get one started. Meanwhile, his stomach began to growl, and he pulled some jerky from a pocket and began to chew on that.

Dan Barber and his riders easily followed the careless sign left by the Sampsons and the Indians. Barber was thankful for that, but he was also made fearful for Anne's safety. He would never have admitted it to another, but he was suddenly grateful Golden was the man she was with. Scott Golden was a man who could handle trouble.

As for Anne, he had no idea what to do with her. The girl had become impossible. And she no longer had any concern about what such a stunt as she had pulled would mean to Barber's friends and neighbors.

If she were ten again, he would put her across his lap and spank her. He frowned at that thought, remembering that he hadn't done that when she was ten and misbehaved.

Impatient, he spurred the gray, pulling ahead to ride alongside Bender. "How far ahead are they?" he asked.

"Several hours."

"Can't you speed up a bit?" Barber asked.

"Need to save the horses," Bender replied. "Rough going now, but be rougher later. Horses play out, we'll never catch up."

There was no arguing with that conclusion, and Barber dropped back to lead Tremble and the men.

"I've never been up this high before," Barber remarked to Tremble, more to take his mind off Anne and the danger she might be in than from any interest in the mountainous terrain.

"I suspect Bender's been all over these mountains," Tremble replied. "Even if we were to lose old Manaqui's trail, he'll know how to locate it again."

"What brought that old Indian and the Sampsons together?" Barber wondered aloud.

"Rifles, I guess."

"Rifles?"

"Sampson supplies guns to Manaqui," Tremble said, "and they both have had run-ins with Golden. I guess they got together because they needed each other to bring Golden to heel."

They rode in silence for a few minutes, but Barber's face was wrinkled with thought. "I guess I made some mistakes bringing up my daughter," he finally said.

"Mistakes?" asked Tremble.

"I let her have her head too much."

Tremble laughed. "You did no such thing, boss. I admit you spoiled her. Me too. But there was nothing you could have done to change her from what she is now."

"What're you saying?" Barber asked, some slight reprimand in his voice.

"I'm saying she's a smart woman who has a mind of her own. She won't let you or anybody else tell her who she's going to marry. Boss, you might as well make up your mind to that."

"We'll see."

Barber had spoken softly, but his jaw had tightened.

Chapter Fifteen

For the next day or so their diet consisted of nuts and berries and a rabbit that Scott managed to knock over with a rock. Even so, Anne gradually grew stronger, and the puppy, which gulped down any morsel Anne offered, grew stronger and sleeker as well.

As the dog filled out, Golden realized he was older and bigger than he had at first assumed. His big feet indicated he would be a large dog when he was grown. Soon he was scampering along at Anne's feet. The companionship of the dog seemed to give Anne strength and, though the pace was slow, she traveled with no help from Scott.

Despite Anne's condition, they could have made the high valley, their eventual destination, in half the time. But first they had to lose those who followed. That was going to be difficult, Scott knew. Still, he was a skilled woodsman and knew these mountains as well as Manaqui and certainly better than the Sampsons.

He had to use that knowledge to lose them. But that would take time.

Whenever possible they traveled over rock or removed their boots and waded up streams, coming out on rock. When there was no rock, he broke off a leafy limb and dragged it behind to brush out any tracks, scattering loose sand and dust over the trail. But even that was meaningless unless the wind or rain helped out, for old Manaqui surely knew every trick.

Along the way he left plenty of false signs, often no more than a brush dragged across a stretch of sand to make it look like an attempt to cover their tracks. A half footprint, a very subtle indentation, pointing north or east suggested they might have made a run in any direction.

When they lit a fire to cook at night or merely to ward off the cold, Scott gathered the coals and buried them before departing, leaving the spot clean with no sign that a camp had ever been made there. When possible, they traveled along animal trails. Knowing that deer and mountain sheep often traveled back and forth over the same trail, he hoped they might destroy any sign of human passage before old Manaqui had a look.

Thus, he finally brought Anne into the high valley.

The cave, one aspect that had held him in the valley when Scott first discovered it, was located in a cove sheltered from view by tall fir and low, scrubby pine. Deep beneath an overhang of granite, wind and snow seldom penetrated to the mouth of the cave. Still, Golden had woven a tight screen of small limbs to cover the mouth and help keep the cold out. He would do the same again, if they had to stay through winter.

"I expect you need some rest," he said to Anne, indicating the bench of rock he had once used for a bed. Some of the grass he had used for bedding was still there, and mice had obviously found the grass convenient for nesting. The wood he had left behind was untouched, and he used one of the precious matches to light a fire. Then turning to Anne, he asked, "Would you have a pin on you?"

"Sure." She produced one from somewhere within her clothes.

He'd had the use of a rifle during his first sojourn here, and he recalled the hides he had turned to leather for clothes, shoes, and other uses. He had used a rock in the rear of the cave for his work bench. He went there now. On the floor around the rock were several short strips of leather. They were so dry and hard they were ready to break when he tried to bend them. Gathering a handful, he went back to where Anne lay. She was already sleeping, the dog by her side. Putting another stick on the fire, he left the cave without disturbing her and, for some strange reason, a little resentful of the dog.

A small lake covered the lowest part of the valley, kept filled by drainage from the higher peaks that showed patches of snow even in summer. He had often wondered how the trout got there, but he had been thankful they had, for they had once provided him with food when he could find no other.

He placed the leather strips in the edge of the water. While they soaked, he looked around. The valley ran east and west. Maybe a mile in width, it was five miles long, at least. From where he stood, Golden saw plenty of animal sign. The pointed prints of mountain sheep were most frequent, and a mountain lion had watered nearby as well. He had even seen an elk this high up a couple of times. With a rifle he had easily survived here. Without one? It wouldn't be easy, he knew.

Soon the water had softened the strips, and Golden tied them into a string. Then, shaping the pin into a crude hook, he kicked among some dry grass and disturbed a black beetle. With the beetle struggling on his hook, Scott threw it out into the water. A moment later he had a nibble. He waited until the fish had plenty of time to swallow the bug, knowing that anything less would drag the crude hook from the fish's mouth. Then he pulled.

He caught two half-pound trout and returned to the cave. Burying them in the edge of the fire's ash, he sat back and waited for them to cook. A few minutes later, he woke Anne, and they ate.

"How long were you here before?" she asked, peeling the white flesh of the fish from the bone and offering some to the dog.

"A year, maybe a little more."

"This is a pretty lonely place," she said. "What did you do all that time?"

"I had a couple of books. I killed my meat and made my own clothes and shoes from the hides. A man shouldn't live off meat alone, so I searched the valley for greens and roots. I also gathered some nuts. Once I followed a brown squirrel to his hideout and stole his."

"Shame on you!"

He laughed. "If I remember correctly, he had plenty of time to gather more. He survived, for I saw him again come spring."

She glanced at him over the fire and met his gaze for a moment. Her eyes dropped first. "You're a strange man, Golden," she said.

Scott didn't respond, not sure he wanted to know more of what had caused her to make such a comment.

"I'm thirsty," she said, rising.

"We'll go down to the lake."

She paused just beyond the cave and looked around. She had seen the valley on their arrival, but she had been tired and hungry. Now she studied the surroundings that had held this strange man here for so many months. Or was it more than the place? Was it something within him? Hadn't he lived almost like a hermit on his ranch? Yes, this high-up place was beautiful, and she tried to understand why this man who had done so much for her had loved the valley.

An eagle soared overhead, circling above the peaks. She thought she heard his cry as the wind stirred the leaves of a nearby aspen, causing them to shimmer and murmur. Anne felt a quiet serenity, a freedom, she couldn't recall feeling before. Was that the allure of this place for him?

"Will the Sampsons find this place?" she asked.

"They'll do their best, and that old Indian is canny. But we'll try and be ready for them if they come."

"With your only weapon a knife and they with guns?"

"There are many ways of fighting," he said. They strode to the lake and drank, cupping their hands to lift the water to their lips.

"Where are those greens and roots you talked about?" Anne asked.

"See that?" He pointed to a fern. "That's called bracken. The roots can be boiled and eaten. They're starchy and salty, and cooked to a mush they're quite tasty."

"Give me your knife."

"I'll dig them."

"Golden?"

"Yes, Ma'am."

"Will you let me do something for myself, and please, call me Anne?"

"Yes, M—Anne."

Golden watched as she dug out several of the dark, cord-like roots. "Now where are the greens?"

"You can use the bracken tops as greens when they're young. They're a kind of asparagus." He pointed to a few remaining sprouts. "Gather these. You'll need to soak them overnight before you cook them."

"I'll need some kind of pot to soak them in," she said. "And something to cook them in as well."

"There's some soft soapstone on the other side of the lake. I made pots from it. You can't set them on the fire. They get too hot and crack. But you can set them near and turn them from time to time. It's awfully slow cooking, but it works."

"You make me a pot," she said, "while I gather

more of the sprouts and clean these roots. Tomorrow we'll have potatoes and greens with our fish."

Without discussion, the workload divided itself along certain lines between them. Golden taught Anne what herbs, roots, and leaves to gather and told her how to cook them. He also pointed out the ones that could be dried and kept for winter, urging her to harvest plenty of those. He cautioned her to cover over where she dug and leave no sign.

"If someone comes into the valley, we don't want them to know anyone is here," he warned.

Fish were plentiful in the lake, and he caught more than they could eat. Those that weren't eaten he cleaned and gutted and hung in the sun to dry.

They had firewood to gather as well. Having no axe, the only choice was to find fallen trees whose limbs they could break into pieces and carry back to the cave.

Gathering wood required as much time as gathering and cooking food, and all their preparation might go for naught if the Sampsons came, Golden reminded himself frequently. But not to prepare for winter would be foolish.

Often he left Anne to her work, and took long treks down the eastern slopes to scout for sign, gathering pockets full of nuts when he found them. On one of these hikes he came across a patch of young, slender scrub oak. He had been looking for these to make a bow and arrows. He had not hunted with a bow and arrow for many years, and hoped he hadn't lost his skill. But he could practice, and if he could fashion a proper one, he'd be better prepared for the Sampsons if and when they showed up. With a bow and arrows he could also hunt for larger game.

He cut several young oaks, all of which were right for the bow. Several smaller ones he cut for arrows, selecting only the straightest. There would be no stone or metal on their tips, but the oak would be hard when seasoned. He returned to the valley, hoping he had enough leather for bowstrings.

He cut the various pieces of oak into the proper lengths, and while the smaller lengths were still green, he sharpened one end into a point. Each morning he took them from the cave and placed them in the sun, bringing them in at night and placing them near the fire. He had two strips of leather long enough for bow-strings. Wetting these, he rolled and twisted them into strings, after which he worked grease from their cooking into the leather cord.

When the wood was finally dry and seasoned, he put the strings on the two bows, reached for a couple of arrows, and walked outside to try them. Anne followed and stood some distance away to retrieve the arrows. Often the arrows did not fly straight, but Golden would shoot at only large targets, like animals and, possibly, men.

"May I try?" Anne asked, after several attempts by Scott. He offered her a bow and stepped back to watch. She fitted the arrow to the string expertly and let fly. Golden was surprised at the distance.

"You've done this before," he said, after she had repeated the same feat a few times.

"Back east in school. It was part of our outdoor exercise. My favorite part, as a matter of fact."

After that they practiced an hour or so each day. From time to time geese flew in to settle on the lake, and Golden began to stalk them, bagging one occasionally, but more often losing an arrow. Thus, on another scouting excursion, he returned to the patch of oaks. He still had several lengths for bows, but he needed more arrows.

He never returned to the valley by the same route, a practice he had learned long ago when he had barely escaped an ambush from a poor loser in a poker game. On this occasion during the circuitous route he chose, he came upon a fresh camp. Several Indians had spent the night there and at least three white men. The Sampsons, he thought to himself, And they were close, he realized. Very close.

He thought of Anne and felt a hot lurch deep in his belly. He had been away for several hours now. What if they had found the valley? Abruptly, he turned and ran, crashing through brush he ordinarily would have gone around. If something had happened to Anne . . .

His special valley didn't seem so beautiful anymore.

Chapter Sixteen

The one from whom he had most to fear was the old Indian. Scott found that ironic. He'd never before had an argument with an Indian, and had never killed one. In fact, he had been called "Indian lover" more than once. He took some pride in that at a time when white men claimed that the only good Indian was a dead Indian. Now he felt sure he'd have to kill old Manaqui.

His thoughts traveled back to the wizened old Indian whose life he had once saved. That had happened somewhere in the Cherokee Strip after he'd ridden out of Cimarron.

The strip had lived up to the descriptions Scott had heard. The country was not a desert, but the rolling hills were brown and dry and free of trees except along the bottoms of ravines, where a little water collected during the infrequent rains. Except for an occasional small settlement, the land was as free of people as trees, except for the outlaws. Since there was no law in the Strip, outlaws from Montana to Texas had taken refuge there. Any lawman who entered the Strip knew there was more than a good chance he'd never leave it alive.

Scott had ridden into the small settlement known as Wheaton an hour before dark, and pulled the piebald to a stop. Looking the place over, he had seen a long, weather-beaten building with a sign reading Wheaton General Merchandise. The Silver Dollar Saloon and five or six dwellings made up the rest of the settlement. He pulled up before the saloon, stepped down, and tied the piebald and his pack pony to the hitch rail alongside three other horses.

Pushing through the swinging doors, he stepped sideways so as not to be outlined by the light from behind, and waited for his eyes to adjust to the dimness of the room. The saloon was a square room, maybe forty by forty, and the bar ran across the back. Three men, probably the owners of the horses outside, stood propped against the bar with drinks before them. All three turned to inspect Scott as he approached the bar and took a position several feet from where they stood.

All three were large and dark-complexioned, and dressed in range garb. They wore tall black Texas hats and tied-down six-guns. They looked so much alike Scott decided they had to be brothers.

"What'll you have?" asked the bartender, a slender man with very pale skin, suggesting he saw little of the sun.

"I'll have a glass of water," Scott said, "and I'll be glad to pay."

"No charge," the bartender said, turning away and pouring water from a metal jug on the shelf behind the bar.

The three men down the bar, hearing the exchange, guffawed loudly, and made what were obviously unpleasant remarks, though Scott couldn't hear them.

"I thought I might stay over for the night. Is there some place I could rent a bed?" Scott asked the bartender.

"We ain't got no hotel, if that what's you mean."

"Maybe a boardinghouse where a man could get a good meal?"

"Well, there is the widow Sloan. She takes in boarders from time to time. She might have an empty bed."

"Where could I find Mrs. Sloan?"

"I can point out her place, if you want to step up to the front with me," the bartender said, coming from behind the bar. "By the way, my name is Rufus Blount."

"Scott Golden."

"Don't recall seeing you around here before," Blount said.

Scott remained silent.

"See that house over there?" Blount asked, indicating the dwelling farther along the dusty expanse of street. "That's Widow Sloan's. She's also a good cook. I've never eaten there. But everybody says it's true."

"Would she have a corral where I could leave my horses?"

"The barn's behind her house. You could leave them there, I guess. It's been vacant since old man Sloan died some months back." He glanced over his shoulder at the three men at the bar. "Be careful about them," he said, keeping his voice low.

"Who are they?"

"The Garner brothers. Ain't a meaner crew in the Strip. They're wanted in Texas for murder, and they've been run out of Kansas and Nebraska for rustling and stage robbery. Left a lotta dead bodies behind, I'm told."

As they turned to re-enter, an elderly man came from behind the saloon. Scott saw at once he was Indian. His clothes were in tatters, and he wore a beat-up old felt hat.

"Oh, no!" Blount said when he saw the Indian.

The old man seemed not to notice them, though he had to push past them to enter the saloon.

"Comes in here every day wanting whiskey, but never has any money," Blount said. "The boss has ordered me to cut him off, so I can't give him any even if I wanted to."

The old man stood quietly at the bar until Blount returned. "You know I can't give you a drink, Charlie," Blount said, stopping before the old man.

The old Indian made no reply, appearing not to hear Blount. He simply stood before the bar and continued to eye the bottles of amber liquid.

"Now get along, Charlie. You're disturbing my customers," Blount said wearily.

Scott, who had returned to the bar, couldn't help but pity the old man. His face was wreathed in wrinkles, eyes red and watery, and his lips had begun to tremble. Still, the old Indian made no move to leave the bar.

"I'll get the dirty old skunk outta here," said the nearest Garner brother. Striding to where the old Indian stood, he seized the old man's collar and threw him to the floor. "Now git!" he commanded.

The old man either couldn't or didn't move, and Garner kicked him soundly in the ribs.

"Don't do that!" Scott said, appalled at such an act and angry as well.

Garner turned and stared at Scott as if he couldn't believe what he had heard. "Who are you?" he asked belligerently, eyeing Scott's six-gun, his hand resting on the butt of his own.

Scott had no intention of backing down. Cruelty was something he couldn't abide. Garner had had no reason to assault the old man.

"Who I am doesn't matter," he said, facing Garner. "Just leave the old man alone."

He read the intent in the man's hooded eyes a second before he went for his gun, and Scott was ready. As Garner's hand dropped, Scott drew, aiming for the left of Garner's chest. Scott's gun exploded before Garner's was free of leather. A loud grunt escaped Garner as he grabbed at air for support, then, dropping his gun, sank to his knees and then to the floor.

With half an eye on the gunman on the floor to make sure he didn't rise again and the rest of his attention on the other two Garners, Scott dropped his six-gun back into the holster. Then he spoke to the two brothers who stared at the fallen man, looking as though they couldn't believe what had happened.

"Don't take a hand in this," Scott said, sensing they were about to draw. "Just take your brother and get out of here."

The remaining brothers hesitated a moment, their eyes fixed on Scott's gun. Then both went for their guns at the same instant. Scott drew leather again, and shot the nearest, whose gun was only halfway out of the holster. The other, having more time, had his gun out. Scott stepped aside before the man squeezed the trigger, and the bullet burrowed into a wall.

"Don't try it again!" he cried, but the man turned the gun on him again. Scott's bullet caught him in the neck, and the man staggered back, blood seeping through the hand that he had raised to the wound.

The old Indian still lay where he had fallen. Scott knelt beside him and asked, "You all right?"

The old man muttered something that Scott didn't understand, but he began to push himself up, Scott giving him a hand.

"Give him a drink on me, Rufus," Scott said.

Rufus Blount poured a generous drink and passed it to the old Indian, who held it between trembling hands and lifted it to his lips. Then he set the glass on the bar, turned, and shuffled out of the saloon.

"Didn't even thank you," Blount said.

"No matter." Scott reached for his glass of water and finished it off.

"More?" Blount asked.

"No thanks."

"I never saw a faster draw," Blount said, studying Scott. "Should I know you?"

"I was lucky," Scott said. He placed a gold piece on the bar. "For three boxes for those gents and the rest for someone to dig a hole for them," he said. "That is, if you can find someone who can stand the sight of them."

"Guess that'll have to be me," Rufus Blount said. "How long you planning to stay in town?"

"Not long."

Scott chased that ancient scene from his mind. "I better think on what's before me rather than the long-forgotten past," he muttered aloud, and hoped he wasn't too late, that the Sampsons and old Manaqui hadn't found the valley. But he hadn't heard any barking, and surely the dog, who was devoted to Anne, would have given the alarm if someone came near.

Chapter Seventeen

He found Anne safe, plaiting a grass mat for the floor of the cave. Telling her what he had found, he asked her to give him her word she wouldn't stray from the cave until he returned.

"Keep the dog close by. I'll come back as soon as I can."

"You're going out looking for them, aren't you?"

"I have to."

"How long will you be gone?" she asked.

"Till I find them. We can't sit and wait for them to find us."

"What will you do then?"

"I don't know. Might depend on how close they are."

"Be careful, Scott."

He loved the sound of his name on her lips, and stood for a moment savoring it.

"Anything else?" she asked softly.

Her question brought him back into the moment. Did she ask for more than just advice about what she should do if their enemies came? He couldn't imagine that she did. "Not that I can think of," he said and turned away.

The sun dropped behind the western horizon as he left the valley. Stopping, he took a moment to enjoy what was always a beautiful spectacle. One moment the rays stretching up the darkening sky were lemon yellow, then darker gold, and finally a brilliant orange. The last edge of the sun, before it disappeared, was blood red. He doubted there were more beautiful sunsets in the world than when one watched them from the top of the earth.

By the time he returned to the spot where he'd found the camp, darkness was setting in. Still, there was enough light to follow such an obvious trail for a time. He was relieved to find they had headed northerly and might not come up on the valley. They might, however, turn south again.

The darkest time of day was after twilight had passed and before the stars came out. During that period, thirty minutes or so as it turned out, Golden sat and waited, chewing on some jerked goose. When he could see the trail again, he set out. Feeling the ground through his moccasins before his feet touched down, he avoided any sound of breaking twigs or the rustle of grass and leaves. Still, he traveled surprisingly fast. Every sense was alert for the smell of smoke or an alien sound, especially for any moving shadow among the dark rocks and trees. Once a large animal, maybe a wolf, bounded away, causing Golden to freeze for a moment.

The moon rose, the only suggestion that time was passing, but Scott had become so involved in the task before him he had given no thought to time. He had been on the trail for several hours when he caught the first faint whiff of smoke. He was now at least ten miles south of the valley, so he knew the smell didn't come from there. Going even more cautiously as the smell grew stronger, he searched for a glimpse of flame. Finally, he found a strange sight in a bowl around a small spring.

Two fires burned within the bowl.

Carefully inching his way to within fifty yards of the camp, he saw that the Indians had one fire, with old Manaqui occupying the most prominent and warmest spot. The Sampsons, dominated by the old patriarch, lay about the other. Did the separation suggest there might be some division between the two groups? Scott wondered, and then decided it didn't.

Golden lay quietly and tried to think what to do. He heard the snort of a horse nearby and thought of scattering their mounts. But old Manaqui would surely be more careful than that. No doubt he would have posted a guard, maybe two. What else? He might make his way to the Sampsons' fire. He could take out one with the knife before the others woke but no doubt their guns lay close at hand. Could he escape before they shot him? He wasn't at all sure he could. In fact, the odds were very much against it, and he could undertake no risk that might leave Anne alone.

As he lay and continued to consider the situation,

the first vestiges of dawn appeared in the sky, and Golden slipped quietly away, hiding among some brush and rocks a hundred yards from the camp. He was tired and sleepy now that he had found his prey and, assuming the fetal position for warmth, he slept.

The first stirrings in the camp woke him. The fires were renewed, and soon the smell of frying bacon and boiling coffee drifted out to Scott. His stomach roiled with hunger, and he found another strip of jerked goose and chewed on that.

Golden was too far away to hear their talk, except for a word now and then. Everyone seemed at ease, with no apparent concern that their presence might be known.

Even old Manaqui, of necessity a very cautious man, seemed calm and relaxed. The old Indian was a fool if he trusted the Sampsons, Golden thought, but maybe he felt secure because his band far outnumbered theirs.

When Jonathan Sampson had eaten, he pushed himself up and took a few strides from the camp. Looking around, he called back to the fire. "Get up and come here, Champ," he called.

"What for, Pa?

"I want you to scout around some."

"Let the Injuns do it, Pa."

"You get up and do as I say!"

Reluctantly, Champ Sampson rose and walked to his father. They appeared to argue for a short time. Scott listened to their exchanges with interest. Champ seemed very close to open rebellion. Was the old man losing control over his sons? That might be an interesting showdown if it ever came, Scott decided, and hoped he might be around to see it.

Finally, Champ agreed with whatever his father wanted him to do and, reaching for his rifle, cut out away from the camp, taking a parallel course to Scott's position. He's going out to scout around. Here's where I might get my chance at him, Scott thought to himself.

Scott slipped from his hiding place and gradually closed in behind Sampson. Champ stopped frequently to listen, which allowed Scott to close the gap between them and finally, pass him. Stepping behind a large spruce, he waited for Champ to approach, already set on what he would do. When Champ was even with the spruce, Golden stepped out to face him, the distance between them no more than a few feet.

Surprised, Champ came up short. He seemed to collect himself, and then swiftly brought his rifle up for a shot. Stepping in, Golden swept the rifle aside with his left hand. Almost at the same instant, he slammed a right blow to Sampson's chin. Sampson was thrown backward, dropping the rifle as he hit the dirt. He lay there staring up at Scott.

"Get up!" Golden said quietly. "Or don't you want to take me on when I'm able to fight back?"

Scott's voice held a mocking challenge. Champ couldn't resist the chance to prove himself and impress the others by taking out Golden. The former boxer rose warily and faced Golden. He glanced at the rifle, and seemed to decide that was too chancy. His hand then hovered over the six-gun strapped around his waist.

"What's wrong with those fists, Champ?" Golden taunted. "I thought you were bull of the woods when it came to a fist fight."

"I'll tear out your heart and stuff it down your throat, Golden," Sampson snarled.

"Come on then! What're you waiting for?"

Sampson's eyes seemed to grow smaller and darker as he glared at Golden. They were old-looking eyes . . . eyes that had looked upon much that was wicked and evil. "I'll beat you to a pulp and turn you over to that old Indian who wants your scalp." He charged, letting out a snarl that sounded like an angry beast's.

Golden stayed where he was until Sampson was almost upon him. Then he took a step forward and planted a right to Champ's chin. Champ merely smiled and continued to advance. Stepping aside, Scott hooked a blow to Champ's belly, his fist sinking almost to his wrists. The big man stumbled a little but righted himself, his arms reaching out for Scott.

Backing away, Scott stumbled over a limb and lost his balance. Looking up, he saw Sampson rushing toward him. Before he could move, the big man stepped in and took a wild swing with his boot, the toe striking Scott in the ribs. Pain knifed through him so sharp as to dull his senses. He managed to draw himself into a ball before the boot struck again.

"Now you git up!" Sampson growled.

But he didn't wait for Scott to comply. Instead, he grabbed the front of Scott's shirt, lifting him upright. Holding Scott at arm's length, he slammed an uppercut to Scott's chin that sent shivers of light racing through his brain. Then he whirled Scott around, slipping his arms about Scott's chest. Sampson gave a mighty squeeze, forcing the air from Scott's lungs.

"I'm gonna break your back," Sampson whispered in Scott's ear. "Then I'm gonna turn you over to them Indians. They want a piece of you." The man's arms were as large as a small man's legs and bulged with muscle as he sought to squeeze the life out of Scott.

Scott knew he had only seconds to come up with something if he wanted to live. His arms were pinned to his sides, but he could still maneuver his hands. Searching along his belt, he felt for the knife, praying he hadn't lost it during the fight. Finally, his hand found the handle and pulled the knife out. With his arms pinned to his sides, the only thing he could do was stab feebly at Sampson's belly. He tried a couple of jabs and felt Sampson's arms loosen a little. That little gave Scott the leverage he needed, and he put all his strength into the final thrust he made with the knife.

There was a loud swoosh as Sampson lost air, but he didn't go completely down. Instead, he grabbed Golden's leg, lifted it high, and flipped Golden on his back. Golden, landing hard, had no time to recover before Sampson, the front of his pants wet with blood, was on top of him again, his hands feeling for Golden's throat this time.

Sampson's huge hands tightened about his neck, and Golden's wind was cut off. Peering down at him, Sampson sneered, convinced he had a death hold on Golden. "You're finished now," he said, "and we'll do what we please with that woman."

His face was now only inches away, and Golden

suddenly brought his head up and smashed into Sampson's nose. There was a crunch as bone gave way, and Sampson's hands came loose.

Golden brought his legs up and clamped them around Sampson's neck. Squeezing hard, he forced Sampson backward and flipped him to one side. He scrambled up and took a moment to catch some badly needed oxygen as Sampson crawled again to his feet. Neither man spoke now as they faced each other. They circled warily and then came together. Sampson landed a right to Golden's jaw that sent stars shooting through his brain. A left followed the right, which might have ended the fight had Scott not slipped the punch. As he did, he brought both fists up and into Sampson's belly. Sampson went to his knees. When he came up he had managed to draw the six-gun.

Scott grabbed the hand that held the gun with both of his and gradually forced it up and back. In the midst of the struggle the gun went off. Sampson's grunt was almost gentle. He remained upright for a moment, folded, and went down. Golden stepped back, prepared for Sampson to rise again. But the man was dead this time, from a bullet that had pierced upward from under his chin.

Scott was stunned, but only for a moment. He had enough sense to know the others would come running when they heard the shot. Grabbing Sampson's six-gun and rifle, he was on the point of flight when he remembered the gun belt. There would be a few bullets in the guns, but he would need more if it came to a fight. Kneeling, he struggled to unbuckle the belt, but the angle at which Sampson lay and his heavy weight kept the belt too tight for him to loosen the buckle.

Already men were crashing through the brush toward him, but he managed to roll Sampson over, freeing the buckle of his weight. Over the prone body, he saw Jonathan and Boyd in the lead and several Indians much farther back. Throwing the gun belt over his shoulder, he grabbed the guns again and ran.

Guns exploded behind him, and bullets kicked up dust at his feet. Something struck his left thigh with the force of one of Champ Sampson's punches. He stumbled and almost went down, then managed to keep running. Glancing back, he saw the two remaining Sampsons kneeling over Champ's body.

The pain immediately subsided. Scott figured that he had probably been knicked by a rock that was hit by a bullet. He picked up his pace again and was out of sight by the time the Indians caught up to the Sampsons. Several minutes later, he paused for a second to listen for pursuit. He strapped on the gun belt and holstered the pistol.

Whatever he did, he mustn't lead them anywhere near the valley. In fact, he needed to take them even farther away. He felt he would be more than a match for them among the steep cliffs and narrow passages he knew so well.

Golden thought of one place in particular, a narrow ledge that wound around a tall peak, which only he and a few mountain sheep had ever traveled. If he could lead them to that peak, he could climb that ledge and maybe lose them. They'd be several miles from the valley then. Having made his decision, he turned in a southerly direction, making sure he left sufficient sign for old Manaqui and the Sampsons to follow.

The slopes were host to tall pines with thick brush underneath. As he pushed his way through the tangled briars and vines, he heard the angry curses of the Sampsons as they fought through the tangled brush, and he had to smile at their discomfort. But they had more than once overcome the obstacles he put in their way. He knew better than to think they would become discouraged and give up the chase. And there were the Indians, too.

"Here, Pa! He went this way!" Scott heard Boyd yell, his voice reflecting his glee at finally having Scott so close at hand.

"How do you know?" old Sampson yelled back.

"He's beat the bushes down! There's all kind of sign!"

"Good! We'll kill 'em for sure this time!"

But the Sampsons weren't the source of Scott's real fear. He felt certain he could outmaneuver them. Old Manaqui and his Indians were the real source of danger. He hadn't seen whether they had joined in the chase with the Sampsons or not, but he had to assume they had. Nor had he heard them, but that was when the old renegade would be the most dangerous.

Scott was sweating profusely now. He could feel huge drops as they ran down his face, feel the wetness beneath his arms and down his back. More serious was his shortness of breath, and he tried to drag huge gulps of the thin mountain air into his lungs. Glancing to the east, he was surprised to see that the sun was well into the sky, and he wondered where the time had gone. He wondered about Anne as well. If he didn't get back to her soon, she'd think the worst. There was no telling what she might do then.

Suddenly, the trees thinned, and before him loomed the peak he sought. The first several feet were little more than loose shale knocked loose from the cliff above by wind and rain, but he had no time to worry about whether he could make it up the slope or not. The shale slowed him some, but finally he reached the solid rock higher up.

Then he came to the ledge. He had forgotten just how narrow and slick the passage was. He took a moment to strap the bullet belt about his waist and, carrying the rifle under one arm, he pushed on, wondering if either the Sampsons or the Indians would dare follow him up the slick rock. That they might not was a satisfying thought.

Then something smashed into the rock just above him, showering him with dust and small stones. An instant later came the crash of the explosion. A second shot followed immediately, but this time Scott had no idea where the bullet hit, since he felt no shattering rock. He could only hear the ricocheting echoes that beat back and forth against the cliff and the trees below.

He continued to scramble up the ledge and, glancing down, caught sight of the Sampsons. They had emerged from the thick growth and stood at the base of the shale looking up. Boyd was doing the shooting. As he lifted his rifle for a third shot, the ledge curled around a large shoulder of rock, and Scott made the turn before Boyd could get the shot off.

The Sampsons can't make that climb, Golden thought to himself. Boyd was too clumsy and his father too old. Scott was not so sure about the Indians. Still, he knew he had no choice but to return to the valley to make sure Anne was all right. With that in mind, he began his descent from the high peak, taking a roundabout route, hoping to evade the Sampsons as well as old Manaqui.

The more he thought about Anne the more nervous he became. He had been away from the valley far too long. Maybe his concern made him careless, or maybe he had underestimated the Sampsons. Whatever the case, he was unprepared for what happened next. Suddenly a rifle boomed on his left, and something struck his leg with the force of a mule's kick. His leg was knocked out from under him, and he went down. That fall saved his life, for the first shot was followed by a barrage of bullets that slammed savagely into the trees around him, cutting through small limbs and ripping through leaves.

Gripping his rifle in both hands, he used his elbows to drag himself deeper into the trees. He pulled himself along for maybe fifty feet or more. Then he pushed himself up and ran, bending low and ignoring the numbness in his leg.

For the moment there was no pain from the wound, and Golden picked up his pace even more. Several minutes later, he came to a stream and paused for a second to listen. Hearing nothing, he plunged into the water and ran with the current.

Now the pain began, feeling like a hot iron plunged repeatedly into his thigh. But he knew he had to keep running, for they'd be after him soon. If they caught him, what would happen to Anne? He had to get back to her. His left pants leg was soaked with blood, and the water of the stream was briefly red before the current swept the blood away. Scott would have been more concerned for himself had he known just how much blood he was losing.

He still had not checked the load in the two guns, and he pulled up for a moment. The rifle was fully loaded, and he replaced the bullet that had killed Champ Sampson. Holstering the six-gun, he slipped the loop on so as not to lose it. The stream flowed away from the high valley, taking him farther and farther from Anne, but for the moment there was nothing he could do about it. He came to a beaver dam that turned the stream into a wide marshy area. The whack of a beaver's tail caused him to bring the rifle up, ready to fire. Then he saw the animal plunge into the water before the dam.

Golden decided to leave the stream there and angle back toward the valley. He tried to disturb the marsh as little as possible, but it was becoming difficult to keep his left leg from dragging. Glancing back, he was glad to see that, except for some swirls of muddy water, he left little sign. That would settle again soon, he hoped.

When he left the marsh, he gathered grass and cleaned his boots of mud, stuffing the grass beneath a nearby log. He sat on the log to examine the wound. He couldn't see it though his pants leg, but he was aware of the blood running down his leg and squishing in his boot when he moved his foot. Only then did he realize how much blood he was losing and how much he had already lost. The pain was still strong in his thigh, but now it radiated into his belly and seemed to race through his gut.

He knew he mustn't leave any sign of his passing, but the bleeding presented a problem. But what could he do? He was afraid to stop long enough to create some sort of tourniquet. Then he noticed the small vines running along the log. Lifting the knife from the case on his belt, he cut a length several feet long. Then he wound it tightly around his thigh above the wound and tied it off. After a moment the bleeding slowed. Oddly enough, the tightness of the tourniquet seemed to help the pain a little.

He was a hundred yards or so from the stream, but he heard faint sounds of pursuit as they searched its banks. Pushing himself up from the log, he started out again, walking, not running, and always angling back toward where Anne waited.

The wound was a steady throb now, and the pain an extension of that. And steadily Golden grew weaker. He was climbing again, which made the going tougher, but he managed a couple of miles. Knowing he needed rest, and hearing nothing behind him, he looked for a place where he could mount some kind of defense. Armed with the rifle and six-gun now, he would make them pay if they caught up to him.

He climbed a slight rise and came out on a small plateau, the center of which was a jumble of rocks and boulders. Hobbling into the rocks, he settled down and glanced around. He had a clear field of fire in all directions. He sank down, placing his back against a boulder, and closed his eyes. He was tired, weak as water, and his head ached from the pounding by Champ Sampson. He thought of his leg. He could cut the tail of his shirt into strips for a bandage, but since the bleeding seemed to have stopped, he did nothing. Suddenly, his chin dipped to his chest, and he slept.

The sun was low in the eastern sky when Golden woke. For a moment he had trouble remembering where he was and why he was there. When he dredged up the memory of those last hours before he slept, he knew he must have slept through the night. But how had he escaped the Indians? The Sampsons? He had no idea, but he was grateful. He thought of Anne and the danger which might even at this moment threaten her, and knew he had to get to her as fast as he could.

Incredibly, the wound in his leg was no longer very painful. He removed the vine and cut his pants leg off above the wound. When he slit that portion open, he had a wide piece of canvas from which he could fashion a bandage. Ripping off a couple of slender strips for strings, he wrapped the wound firmly and stood.

The leg was stiff, and with his movement came more pain. Spotting a cluster of wild persimmon, he cut himself a crude crutch. He was at least ten miles from the high valley, a distance he would have ordinarily made in half a day or less. With the wound, he would take longer, but he would get there as fast as he could.

An hour of daylight remained when Golden stood on a ridge overlooking the valley and studied the scene below. Low clouds blanketed the sky and hovered low. Golden knew the signs. The first snow of winter was imminent. He shivered a bit and had a passing thought of how much easier it would be to get some big hides for clothing now that he had a gun.

Nothing moved around the lake, which didn't surprise him. Most animals had found other sources of water since humans had moved in. Nor was there movement among the trees that screened the cove and the cave. Golden carried Champ Sampson's rifle in the crook of the arm opposite the crutch, and the six-gun was packed in the holster strapped around his waist. Confident now that he was armed, he let a minute or so pass, and then began a slow descent into the valley, eyes and ears alert.

When he neared the cove, the dog, alert to his presence, appeared. Then came Anne, glancing cautiously from the among the trees.

"Golden!" she shouted when she saw him. "I thought you'd never return." She ran to him and threw her arms about his neck, hugging him tightly. Then stepping back, she looked down at his leg. "Are you all right? What happened?"

Golden was momentarily stunned at her pleasure at his return, and he thought she had never been more beautiful as she stood there, almost in rags, with a droplet of snow glistening in her hair.

"Afraid I had a slight run-in with Champ Sampson," he finally managed, his voice a little creaky, like a machine that hadn't been used in sometime.

"And?"

"He won't bother us any more."

Anne dismissed the death of Champ Sampson as of no consequence. "Come, let me have a look at that leg." She took the crutch, placed his arm about her shoulders, and led him through the trees into the cave. The dog followed, obviously suspicious and worried that his mistress wasn't paying attention to him.

Scott sat on the rock bench that served as a bed as she undid the canvas bandage. "There's no infection," she said, "but the wound needs cleaning."

Several soapstone bowls that they had made sat on the cave floor some distance back. There were several more than Golden remembered, and some had been carefully fashioned, their outsides so smooth they seemed almost glazed. She's been busy, he thought, and watched her return with one of the smaller bowls. Gently, she washed and cleaned his wound.

Golden sat as still as stone as she worked, conscious of the gentle hands on his thigh.

When she was finished, she looked up at him. "That's better." She rose, and taking the bowl, went to the cave exit and tossed the water outside.

A tide of weariness swept over Golden. He tried to keep his eyes open, sure that there was an important reason he should do so. But for the life of him, he couldn't remember what it was. His eyelids felt as heavy as metal washers, and he was no longer in control of them. He curled his hands into fists and rubbed his eyes as he had when a child, but even that was no use. When he took his hands away, his eyes closed and he slept.

*   *   *

"It's morning," Anne said, shaking him awake. "Are you hungry?"

"I could eat a horse," Golden replied. He lifted his feet from the bed and slowly swung his feet to the floor.

"I've only a trout, but it's freshly roasted," she said, offering him the fish in a small bowl.

He stripped the meat from the bones and ate, washing the food down with water from another bowl. "You made these?" he asked, indicating the bowls.

"I needed something to do while you were gone."

When Golden had eaten, she took the bowls away. He watched as she busied herself at the rear of the cave where their food was stored. Then he pushed himself up and put his weight on his injured leg. He was surprised at the difference only a few hours had made. He had heard that high mountain air allowed wounds to heal quicker, and he thought now that it must be true. Still, he walked gingerly as he moved to the mouth of the cave and pushed through the trees.

A couple of inches of snow had fallen during the night, and the valley wore a trackless blanket of white. Weak beams from a high and distant sun reflected off a thin coat of ice on the lake. Would the approach of winter send the Sampsons and the Indians back to the low country? Surely they had better sense than to face the hardships of a high mountain winter.

Regardless of what their enemies did, Golden now knew he and Anne had no choice but to winter in the cave. The way home was far too arduous for him on a lame leg, and he wasn't sure Anne was well enough to undertake the grueling journey even if he were well.

Thankful they had studiously been preparing for winter, he knew there was still time to gather more wood and food. With his rifle maybe he could bag a deer, though he might have to travel to lower ground. Could he manage that on the lame leg? He wasn't sure he could. But food and warmth were the essentials if they were to see spring come again, and Scott knew he must set about adding to the stores they had already collected.

Over his protests, Anne insisted on accompanying him when he left the valley in search of wood. Now the snow was a problem. To keep the valley as free as possible of signs of occupancy Scott found a way up through the trees on the slope that sheltered the cave. He longed for an axe so he could fell some of the nearer trees, but he had to be content with finding fallen trees with limbs he could break into manageable pieces.

The dog, weighing eighty or so pounds, was as big as he would ever be. He was no longer continuously underfoot but, as they collected wood, often circled well out to explore their surroundings and keep watch. He had also allowed Scott to become his friend. Golden was surprised at how much he had come to depend on the animal's watchfulness.

That worried him some, for he remembered a favorite saying of his long-dead father: "Son, never depend on anyone or anything too much, and you'll never be let down. That bit of advice could save your life sometime." There was truth in the saying, for something could happen to the dog.

With the appearance of the Indians and the remaining Sampsons always a possibility, Scott remained constantly vigilant, and he searched carefully for any sign of men wherever he went. Nor was he ever without the rifle and six-gun. He cut a rawhide strip, attached both ends to the rifle, and slipped an arm through the loop when he carried wood.

On their trips for wood, they were forced to wander farther and farther from the valley. On one such trip, they came upon a grove of oak. The ground beneath was free of snow but littered with acorns.

The cold was severe, but Scott slipped out of his shirt, made a crude sack, and scooped it full of acorns.

"I guess they're good to eat," Anne said, watching the harvest.

"Indians eat them all the time, but they're hard to prepare."

"How so?" she asked.

"First, you soak them overnight to get the kernels from the outer shells. Then you shell the kernels. When the meat is dry, it's ground into a meal. I've seen Indian women mix the meal into a dough. They wrap the dough in fern leaves and put them in ashes to bake."

"Did you ever eat any?"

"Some," Scott answered.

"Were they good?"

"Depends on how hungry you are, I guess."

"And we may get pretty hungry this winter," Anne said.

"I wouldn't be surprised."

Chapter Eighteen

Dan Barber grew more and more frustrated. Not only did Bender not push on faster, the weather turned colder, and that in itself was enough to slow the pace even more. The change in weather brought snow as well.

With the exception of Tremble and Bender, the men became soured by the cold and snow. Though they would never say anything to Barber's face, nor in front of Tremble, Barber was sure they had plenty to say to each other when neither he nor Tremble were present.

Among the men, only Tremble ever talked to him about Anne, and Barber appreciated his foreman's feelings about her. On several occasions, in an effort to comfort him, the aging cowboy had pulled up beside Barber to express his concern.

"We'll find her, and she'll be all right," Tremble insisted. "If she had to be in a situation like this, I can think of no better man for her to be with than Scott

Golden. He's done killed half of them Sampsons and plenty of them Indians. The wonder is that what remains of either bunch has the guts to keep following after the man."

"He'll do his best," Barber replied. "I'm sure of that. But who knows what will happen when they catch up to Golden? My hope is that we catch up to those rascals first."

The severe conditions made Barber begin to feel his age. He had to force himself out from the blankets each morning, and when he was up, he had to walk off the stiffness in his creaking joints. "Like some old fool tottering with age," he muttered, making sure he was out of the earshot of any of his men, including Tremble.

But though Bender refused to set the all-out pace Barber wanted, they still gained on the Indians and the Sampsons. Even Barber, no tracker of any note at all, could see the sign was fresher, and it was easier to follow now that there was snow on the ground. But as they came up closer to the party ahead, Bender became more cautious, which slowed them more. But Barber could understand and appreciate what was in the tracker's mind now. They'd come too far to ride into an ambush and get themselves killed.

Then he saw Bender's hand go up, the signal for those behind. Dropping from the saddle he went on ahead several yards, climbing a slight rise. He lay on his belly, removed his hat, and peered at something beyond the rise. Then pushing himself backward, he stood and signaled the others to come forward.

"We're coming up to them," he said when Barber stood beside him. "You follow me."

Together they repeated the same maneuver that Bender had demonstrated.

"I don't see anything," Barber protested, inspecting the valley carefully.

"See them trees over yonder?" Bender pointed to some trees directly across the valley from where they lay.

"Yes."

"Look above the trees," Bender said. "See that smoke? Ain't much, but it's there."

"I see it" said Barber. "Are you telling me Sampson and those Indians are in there among those trees?"

"No. Look there," the tracker said, pointing to the right, across Barber's body. "Indians and Sampsons go that way. That smoke coming from cave is Golden's smoke. Him and Miss Anne must be in that cave."

"But why did those scoundrels take the long way around?"

Bender sighed. His expression suggested he might as well be talking to a baby. "They're going to attack. If they cut across the valley, they be out in the open. They'd make a fine target for Golden's guns."

"But we've got to help!"

"We will, but we cannot stop the fight from starting," Bender said. "That will happen very shortly."

The first warning that something was wrong was given by the dog. He had been lying near the fire, but growled and raced for the front of the cave, the hair on his neck standing.

"You stay here!" Scott ordered Anne and, grabbing his rifle, ran after the dog.

The first man to appear before the cave entrance was an Indian. He was barely discernable in the dim light from the fire. Scott dropped to his belly, brought the rifle to his shoulder and fired.

Three others followed close behind, and behind them Scott caught sight of Jonathan and Boyd Sampson. They pumped several shots into the cave, and the bullets screamed as they careened off rocks and crisscrossed back and forth, buzzing like bumblebees until they dropped harmlessly to the floor.

Scott squeezed off another shot, and another Indian went down. The rest, including both Sampsons, turned and fled back out of the cave.

"Are you all right, Anne?" he shouted.

"Scared half to death, but I'm fine," Anne shouted back.

"You stay where you are! I'm going after them!" Scott turned and ran, the dog behind him.

An eerie silence descended on the cave after Scott had gone. The smell of spent gunpowder was strong, and smoke drifted toward the small opening high in the top of the cave above.

Anne tried to follow Scott's order and remain behind, but something inside her compelled her to leave the cover of the rocks and follow after Scott and the dog. As she passed one of the dead Indians, she reached down and picked a cloth from his shoulders. The rag smelled like smoked fish and tallow, an aroma that made her feel she might be sick, but she draped it about her own shoulders anyway.

* * *

Boyd Sampson had scrambled wildly from the cave and crashed through the trees. When he reached the open valley, he took out after the Indians, who were already several yards in front.

Boyd glanced once over his shoulder, looking for his father. He couldn't spot the old man, but he did see Scott Golden burst from the trees. Forgetting about his father, Boyd raced even faster after the Indians. He wasn't sure he would make it across the valley and get to the cover of the trees before Golden began to shoot, but he intended to try. Maybe Golden would go looking for Jonathan Sampson and old Manaqui and forget about him.

Suddenly, the Indians turned back. They ran toward Boyd, but their faces were mostly turned back across the valley. Boyd saw what had turned them back. A line of riders on horseback had come from the trees and were charging after the Indians. In the lead was Bender, the half-breed, and not far behind was Dan Barber, the white-haired old cattleman. Boyd stopped and thought of following the Indians who had just passed him by, but the horsemen were keeping a fast pace as they thundered toward him. Dropping his rifle, he raised his hands high above his head.

The Indians continued to flee and, one by one, were being picked off by the posse. None of the riders saw the two old men who quietly vanished into the trees on the other side of the valley, but Scott spotted them. He didn't know how they got there, but he knew that Manaqui and Jonathan Sampson had to be stopped. Both were dangerous men, men who were driven by a terrible, uncontrolled hatred of their world. As long as they lived, they would remain outlaws and renegades. Someone had to put an end to them, and he might as well try to do it himself.

He waited only long enough to see Anne and her father meet and embrace. The dog was also nearby. Now that Anne was safe, he could turn his attention to Manaqui and Sampson.

Clutching his rifle, Golden ran across the valley and into the clump of trees where he had seen the two men vanish. Their trail was easy to follow. Golden moved quicker than his instincts told him was prudent, hoping that the shots from the still-raging conflict would cover any noise he might make. He came upon a clearing. Fewer than ten feet down from him was a half circle of boulders and rocks. Old Manaqui was sitting on one rock, his back against a boulder, looking out on the scene below him. A rifle lay across his lap. It was an excellent outpost for killing anyone who would be riding back to the Barber ranch.

Golden aimed his rifle at the Indian and then paused. He had tried to make a new life for himself, a life that didn't involve killing. That had certainly not turned out the way he'd planned. Maybe he could take these two killers in alive.

The moment Scott heard the voice from behind, he knew that he had been foolish to hesitate. "Drop the rifle, Golden, and don't turn around."

"If I'm going to die, I want to face my killer." Scott turned and looked into the hateful eyes of Jonathan Sampson.

"I've had enough of you, Golden!"

Golden dropped quickly to the dirt. Samson's rifle exploded. A shout of pain and shock cut the air. Manaqui clutched his chest, looked to the sky, then seemed to fold gently to the ground.

Samson stood frozen for a moment, his mouth agape. Scott quickly thrust himself up and sprang at Sampson—catching him off balance. The rifle went off once as it was knocked out of Sampson's hands. They rolled over a few times, Sampson still reaching for the rifle.

Both men scrambled to their feet.

Golden launched himself at his opponent. His head landed squarely in Sampson's stomach, knocking the air out of him. The force of Golden's head threw Sampson backwards. He landed against a boulder, and his head snapped back, colliding with its hard surface. A look of terror and pain passed momentarily over his face. Then he began a slow slide down the boulder. Dropping the rifle at last, he lay beside the big rock, his eyes staring vacantly into the sky.

Scott took a moment to get to his feet. Then he slowly approached the spot where Sampson lay. One look in the old man's eyes was all he needed. Jonathan Sampson's hate was finally played out.

Scott Golden looked away and closed his eyes. "Lord, please, let this be the last man that I kill," he whispered.

He opened his eyes with a strong feeling that his prayer had been answered.

Epilogue

"I can't deny he's a fine man, daughter," Dan Barber said. "But are you sure you want to marry him?"

Father and daughter sat at the table in the large dining room of the Barber ranch house, a cup of coffee before each of them. Beyond the back door, a gust of wind shook the brown leaves of the chinaberry tree and sent them cascading to the ground. Beyond the tree, a high westering sun seemingly smaller than usual, suggested the approach of winter.

"I love Scott, Papa," Anne said and smiled. "I never met a finer man, present company excluded, of course. He'd give his life for me, and you know it."

"I reckon he's already proved that, sure enough," Barber replied. "Still, I hate to lose you. What'll I do in this big house by myself?"

"Scott and I will be only a half day away. You can always come and visit us. You've got plenty of dependable help here."

182

"Yeah, Tremble runs this place better than I can. But why couldn't you and Golden move in here? I'd look upon him as a son."

"You'll have to give him some time, Papa. Scott's been a loner most of his life, and he made a home in his valley. Marrying me and taking me there is a big step for him right now. But you will always be welcome there. He's told me as much." Hearing the clop of a horse's hoof from the front of the house, Anne rose. "That must be him now, so you be nice to him, Papa."

"I will, daughter, I will."

Anne reached the porch and watched Scott step from the saddle and wrap Big Red's reins about the hitch rail. When he stepped up on the porch to face her, she slipped her arms about his neck and kissed him on the lips. She felt the thrill of his touch as his arms went around her waist and brought her close to him.

"I made fresh coffee. Papa and I are having some. Come in the dining room and I'll pour you a cup."

"Sounds like just what I need," Scott said and followed her inside.

"Mr. Barber," Scott said when they entered the kitchen.

"Sit, Scott," Dan Barber said, a little stiffly.

Scott sat across from his future father-in-law and Anne brought a cup of steaming coffee and set it before him.

"How is the work going at the ranch?" Barber asked after a moment.

"Fine when I left," Scott replied. "Thanks for lending me so much help, sir. Mr. Tremble knows more about putting up a building than I'll ever learn. I think sometimes I get in his way."

"Is that why you're out riding?" Anne asked and laughed.

"No, he sent me into town for a couple of items. I decided to stop here on my way back."

"At this rate you'll be late getting home," Barber said. "Be happy to have you stay here overnight."

"I thank you sir, but I have to get those things to Mr. Tremble."

"Well, you and the men be here well before three o'clock tomorrow afternoon," Anne said.

Scott Golden lifted his eyebrows in mock confusion. "Why? What happens then?"

"We're getting married, silly!" Anne said. Coming to Scott, she sat on his knee and slipped an arm around his neck. She laughed at the surprise on his face. She was soon silenced, though, by a firm kiss of affirmation from Golden.